FROM A CORNISH LANDSCAPE

by

David   Watmough

LODENEK   PRESS

Padstow, Cornwall

In loving memory of
Mabel Mitter,
my aunt, godmother and friend

© David Watmough - 1975

Printed by St. George Printing Works.
Camborne - Cornwall - Great Britain

Publisher's preface

As a dramatic artist, David Watmough is best known in Canada where he migrated in 1960. His one-man show, in the words of critics, spell-binds audiences from Vancouver to Montreal. Under the auspices of the Canada Council he has performed his work in the U.S.A., Great Britain and West Germany.

His repertoire of monodramas, based on his childhood, youth and adult manhood, grows continually, presenting an astonishing range of experience and emotions. He plunges his audience back into the very times he speaks of: early war-time on a North Cornish farm; the early 1960s, when he returns from his newly-adopted Canada to visit his bereaved mother; a spring-time wedding in the village church; the sour end-of-war years in Cornwall's county town, Bodmin, where he undergoes the less than exhilarating experience of learning the job of reporter on the local newspaper.

Out of such material comes his characters, so very varied and alive, though many in actuality are long dead: living, breathing, seeing, overcome with passions that they cannot understand, regretfully or joyfully recalling their past lives.

On stage, Watmough himself becomes each one in turn. With the aid of no more than a spotlight, a music stand, and an audience upon whose feelings he plays expertly, he builds a world for all to see and touch and hear.

The very success of his performances has perhaps, to some extent, obscured true valuation of him as a writer. These monodramas are intricately planned and deeply worked on. Every effect is calculated and successful; yet under all the professionalism there shines a passion, even (as in the case of all great artists) a veritable obsession, that drives him and his audience along. As one reviewer has put it: 'The Watmough approach is reminiscent of Dylan Thomas — in recalling the shapes, the wonders and the texture of childhood. Both reveal an ear for the idioms of regional speech and its peculiar rhythms and inflexions. And both celebrate language, for its own sake, in a very special way.'

In presenting this selection of some of Watmough's pieces concerning his Cornish childhood and later experiences, we have no hesitation in exposing these works to the reader's cold, calm eye as pure literature. They stand as valid poetic essays, giving us the opportunity to dwell as long as we will on what the author is recreating; and to connect it with what we know of Cornwall as it was then, and is today. He celebrates a vanishing world, and in that respect is portraying a valuable period of history. His first choice of title was 'Pictures from a Dying Landscape', under which for some time he performed his monodamas. But Watmough himself came to realise that far more of his world still exists than he thought possible : in the narrow high-hedged lanes around St. Kew and St. Endellion the same profusion of wild flowers still blooms each year ; in the farmhouses and villages clotted cream is still made and sold ; Cornish pasties, though much more expensive now, are still made by country wives ; the mixed-farmed fields still present, in these days of mechanisation, the same closely chequered designs, swerving and swooping across hills and valleys ; the cliffs are still there, unspoiled, and the wrecks still occur.

This book closes with the question which haunts all Watmough's work : ' How much is one where one is — and how much where one was ?'

The chief character, the seeing ' I ' of these stories, is Davey Bryant, an alter-ego of Watmough himself. But the author warns that these are not to be regarded as pages of his autobiography. Creative fiction is intermingled with fact. Deliberately, it seems to put us off the scent, Davey's relationship with his aunts and uncles, mother, father, brothers changes : the farm they live on changes location. Thus Watmough will not be pinned down and catalogued. But as the illustrations to this volume show, the locations are real ; they existed then, and exist now, though some of the properties have been 'improved', and taken over by newcomers.

The feel of the countryside remains the same and the fiercely-proud independent Cornish life goes on, though now the native Celts mix unashamedly with a seasonal influx of tourists and a mixture of residents ' down from England '. And Watmough himself, returning yearly from Vancouver, sees it all with passion and intense recall, assessing past and present together with irony and love. As he himself says : ' The themes, I hope are universal, but the context is wrought from the Cornwall where I passed my childhood and the Canadian West where I now live and work '.

Donald R. Rawe,
Director,
LODENEK PRESS.

Contents

List of Illustrations

Trading in Innocence

" We must find somethin,' Davey, to put your lizard in."

My cousin Jan shifted the package that Aunt Nora had given us after Sunday morning chapel, native-like, on to his head.

" I know! The rubbish dump. Tis only a little ways. Hell of a lot of jam jars there."

The suggestion was so obviously right, for once there was no discussion. Twenty yards or so along the railway track, past the faded red metal plaque informing us we were on the property of the London & South Western Railway, we clambered down the embankment towards the rubbish dump that lay alongside the lane beyond.

Before we had made a second breach in the railway hedge that day, we could see the evidence of what we sought. Old enamel buckets with the bottoms kicked out; a blue pitcher, with its side seared with rust, a bicycle frame and a miscellaneous collection of cheap pottery shards, a weather-worn collander, bits of wicker chairs, and water-logged furniture with tufts of stuffing poking out - all were scattered between the lane and the stinging nettle foot of the hedge.

But it wasn't this bric-a-brac that held our attention. Not even the gleams and sparkles of glass which probably meant sunlight on jam jars and other bottles. No, when Jan lifted his hand and went " Shshshsh " we saw, simultaneously, what he meant . . . At the far end of the litter-strewn waste-ground was the bent figure of an old man. He had his back to us as he moved slowly, crablike, this way and that, inspecting the objects on the ground about him, but we recognised him at once. Even without the battered felt hat with the dents pushed out so it looked mysterious, warlocky; without the filthy clothes and scarves wrapped tight about his neck in the July heat, we would have recognised that rubbish dump scavenger. For it was Gomer Lane—a familiar if alien figure about such dumps across North Cornwall, from as far north as Launceston, it was said, down to St. Columb and across the moors to Bodmin.

In expanding excitement we glanced at each other. All tramps were thrilling but Gomer Lane was super special. For somewhere on that bent and shuffling person, somewhere amid the layers of ragged garments that covered him from neck to binder-cord tied ankles, dwelt Albert. Albert was an exceedingly large, exceedingly interesting white rat.

Red-eyed, white furred, pink-skinned, Albert induced in me the precisely opposite effects from his unalbino'd kin of the farms. The fleeting sight or scratching sound of **those** currant-eyed, moist-furred and dung-skinned rats that burrowed in the wall behind my bed, slid silently from manure piles outside the stable or bared angry teeth when caught in the steel indentations of a gin, were enough to ice my insides and bring clammy sweat to my forehead. But Albert blotted his brethren out : atoned for their horror in his slow-moving fastidiousness and lordly mien. In Albert my one hatred in the animal world was overcome. For a moment I almost forgot the cool-skinned creature hanging-limp now between my fingers.

"A'ternoon Mr. Lane," said I, licking my lips with nervous anticipation.

"Bravun day, Mr. Lane," lilted my little brother Brian.

"How be 'ee then, Mr. Lane ? " Jan concluded our greetings.

Like a hedgehog unfurling and twice as prickly, Gomer Lane withdrew from his earthward rummaging, turned slowly and eyed us steadily, one and then the other.

"What you young buggers want ? "

"Finding the odd thing, then, Mr. Lane ? " Jan enquired politely.

But Albert was too important, I felt, for that kind of delay.

"Got Albert with 'ee, then, Mr. Lane ?   Can—can us have a look ? "

"Albert's restin'."

"He—he could rest with me, if you like. While you'm busy searchin' and that."

"Maybe us could 'elp of 'ee find something, Mr. Lane ? " encouraged Jan.

2

Bewhiskered, unkempt, shoulder-length hair under the sweat-greased hat, somewhere amid that hirsute profusion, (and it was hard to place their location specifically) two black and beady eyes roved suspiciously.

" You alone then ?"

" Yes we are Mr. Lane," we chorused, even while wondering if one of the various lumpy bulges about his person, was Albert, or some obscene growth germane to tramps and old men.

" What you doin' here then ?" He creaked round then and faced us more or less directly. But I knew those sharp black peepers of his were scrutinizing the lane stretching behind and beyond us.

" We see'd 'ee from the embankment up there," I told him, " and we remembered Albert down to Wadebridge market—that was prettty whiles ago."

" And once outside our school, Mr. Lane," Brian prompted. " You let us see 'un for a penny each."

" I did, did I ? So you want me to wake him up, is that it ? Well . . if it were a penny afore . . what with the price of bran going up . . . "

I could see this was a profitless tack. " We've just come from chapel - all our pennies is gone in the collection. Perhaps we could help you look round here, though. We might - "

The look I got made my words die on my lips.

" What you got in that package then ? I can see tissue paper. Albert likes tissue paper, he does."

" Oh that," said Jan, " that's just a girl's dress. It's new but it's got to be altered or something." It would have been hard to put more disinterest into his tone than Jan managed but it still elicited an immediate and energetic response from Albert's owner.

" A little girl's dress you say ? Oh, Albert and me loves pretty things—here bring it out, why don't you ? Let old Albert and me have a look, eh ? "

There was a hesitation on the rubbish dump, we endeavoured to read each other's faces - but failed.

Gomer Lane rubbed the legs of a primus stove clean against his sleeve with a calming, rhythm. " I was thinking

3

of breeding Albert again—his last litter was beautiful. They all went up to Camelford."

We waited expectantly.

Gomer sniffed. " Costs money to breed you know. Like I had a lovely doe in mind for Albert. You have to pay for that."

" What — what will happen to the babies then ? " — visions of dear little Albert replicas already scampering around my mind. Gomer Lane came close to being airy. He waved the tripod legs of the primus stove. " Oh I shall have to dispose of 'em of course. For a small sum — jest enough to pay for their breeding and raisin'." The brass legs returned to his side. " What you say you got in there ? "

There was no guile in little Brian. " We told you. A girl's dress." My vision quivered alarmingly for fear of Brian's frankness on the old man. " Would you like to see it, Mr. Lane ? Jan, why don't you show him of 'un ? "

Jan's thoughts were evidently pursuing similar patterns to mine. " I was just about to show it to 'ee. 'Ere, this is it." Like a proud shopkeeper displaying his wares, Jan pulled off the lid, spread wide the tissue paper and draped the royal blue length across his arm. " Brand new—just got to be taken in a bit. That's what she said."

" 'Tis worth quite a bit," said Brian, who was given at times to mercenary phrases.

Gomer Lane reached out an age-mottled hand. " Here, let's have a look then."

Jan handed it over and we watched the old man's practised evaluation of such a boring object with grave interest. The dress meant little, Gomer Lane, a great deal, and Albert and his plans of posterity even more.

"Good velvet—for wartime I mean. Of course, 'tis second hand already, you got to remember that. Who's it belong to ?"

Even I was surprised at Jan's speed and firmness of response. " Us," he said simply. " It belongs to us. We was thinking of giving it someone for a present."

" Tis for our cousin, Mary," Brian modified. " Aunty Nora can't alter it, but Aunt Mat can."

Jan, I decided, must have my support. " Tis for her

birthday. We can always get her something else—it isn't till September.

Jan's glance at me was a reward in itself.

"How—how much is Albert's babies going to be?" asked Brian, pursuing his financial considerations.

Gomer glowered at him. "Well, they ain't cheap. I can tell you that, nipper," he said. "He throws a very good litter, does Albert. I reckon his youngsters 'ud make five bob apiece in one o' them there pet-shops, down to Truro say."

"That's a lot, that is," said Brian, screwing up his face to visualize the sum.

With sinking heart, aware I was clutching at straws, I held up my lizard, I'd caught on the railway embankment. "How—how much do you give me for him?"

The effect on Gomer Lane was startling. "Here—keep that away, you hear me? That's a horrible four-legged emmet, that is. Spit poison they do." Even as he spoke the old man was stepping hastily back. One boot crashed heavily through a rusting meat-safe which he kicked savagely free of him. "Bloody thing!" he muttered. Then turned his ire back on me and my offering. "Probably got poison all over your hands from that revoltin' critter, horrible bugger," he said. "Don't 'ee know about four-legged emmets? The green un's?"

Jan had started biology whereas I was still doing nature-study. "Don't worry, Mr. Lane. The only poisonous animals in Britain are adders—no lizards. Really."

"Don't talk nonsense to me, boy. That's a four-legged emmet, a green un. And they can spit a mile at 'ee if you bain't careful. Effect on 'ee for months, 'twill. Bewitchun' creatures they be. Any ol' fool knows that!"

"Will 'ee take the dress in exchange for some of Albert's babies?" I dropped my lizard and didn't even bother to watch it scamper away, so eager was I to see myself a possessor of one of Albert's offspring.

"Ugly brute." Gomer Lane watched my green lizard disappear amid the stinging nettles before responding to my urgently delivered question. "Eh? What was that? This dress—for some of Albert's litter? Well I daresay as how something could be arranged."

"We'd all want one o' course," Jan meditated. "That 'ud be three now, wouldn't it ? "

"Rats have bravun big litters, don't 'em ?" suggested Brian.

Still aware of his superiority of education via the biology class Jan took occasion to think a little more out loud. "Period of gestation, what be that with rats, then ? Twenty-twenty-five days I bide, idn't it ?"

The talk was not to Gomer's liking. "Well, Albert bain't going to provide the whole bloody village with littluns, I don't mind telling you that !!"

"Three babies at five shillings would only make fifteen bob," said little Brian. "Our dress is worth more 'un that, Maister."

"So are you, old fella, aren't you ?" As Albert's head and stout white body suddenly followed a pink sniffing snout out from under one of Gomer Lane's jerseys, the old man's psychological victory over a trio of boys was complete. The pulse of each of us raced as Albert slowly, questingly, made his way up the old man's grimy front, cupped underneath by Gomer's protecting hand.

"Like to give Albert a stroke then ? Go on. He's perfectly tame, likes a bit of a stroke, don't you my lovely."

One by one we moved forward and thrilled to the feel of finger tips on the coarse white coat that rippled under our touch.

"When—" I had to stop and clear my throat of the accumulated excitement "when would they be ready then ? When could we have our babies ?"

"See how he likes that velvet. He likes to snuggle Albert does. 'Smatter of fact if I took this frock it would just be to give him and his youngsters a bed to lie on. Very fond of soft velvet, rats is." Only then would he vouchsafe me a look. "Oh, I reckon I should be passing down this way again in about six weeks time. That 'ud be just about right, wouldn't it ? They'd be just ready to look after themselves I reckon. Beautiful little fellas they'd be by then."

"Here," said Jan, huskily, "you'd better have the box too." And handed it over.

"Mind holding Albert a minute, while I pack this in ?"

6

Gomer Lane looked at us all, fractionally, before handing the squirming weight of Albert into Jan's hands. At once we crowded round Cousin Jan, Gomer Lane, the dress all but forgotten. . .

"Here, Jan try him with this? See if he do like dock leaves?"

"He's fat idn' 'ee? Gosh his tail's clean, idn't it?"

"See they eyes, you. Look, look, he's a-closun of 'em. Old bugger's gin sleep."

"He do like you, that's for sure, Jan.

"Well, Albert, old man. Time we was on our way, eh? Can I have him then, boy. We got a long way to go, Albert and me have."

Our hands and outstretched arms lingered lovingly over the white rat as the transfer took place.

"See you at Highway. I'll come down on the mid-day train. I'll have the youngsters and instructions. Rats like Albert are particular you know. They're thoroughbreds—you gotta remember that."

"When? When?" I asked. "What date will you come?"

"Let's say the middle of next month, shall we? How about the 16th?"

"That's a week and five days before Davey's birthday," Brian explained.

"Good. Then 'twill be a nice birthday present for him, won't it? Well, best be off. Midday I'll be here. I'll be on the noon train from Camelford. Bye then, boys."

We watched him shuffle towards the turnpike, the parcel tight under his arm. As we turned ourselves down the lane Jan and I smiled at one another with satisfaction.

Then little Brian broke our comfortable spell.

"Know what?"

"What?" we chorused.

"I don't think we'm ever gin see that Gomer Lane or his Albert agin."

As we moved forward in unison to push my little brother in the stinging nettles I had a sinking feeling that he would once more be proved right.

He was, of course.

Flies, Lizards and Bonar Law

In the pitch-pined house of worship I sat with my brother Brian and Cousin Jan and read behind the central pulpit that ' Cod ' Is Love and listened to Bonar Law. We knew that God would have been Love if a bit of the G hadn't fallen off, but we didn't know why the lay-preacher from Tintagel was nicknamed Bonar Law—though we were dimly aware that years and years ago, long before we were born that is, some prime-minister in far-off London had that name. Maybe he looked like our fisherman advocate of salvation, maybe he sounded like him. It was enough that father, even grandfather always said that Bonar Law was down for the third Sunday in the month on the North Cornwall Methodist Circuit—and we could then exchange grins of anticipation for Bonar Law with his fiery earnestness made our Sunday Morning at the Turnpike Chapel more pleasurable than did any of his brethren.

This morning, though, this July morning when the blue-bottles buzzed frantically above their dead and dessicated kin on the window sill, we of the three front Sunday School pews had more than Bonar Law for our delectation.

Only intermittently did we give ear to the voice above the panelled lectern. And that when we felt that it was us rather than the three or four farmers, a half-dozen wives and a sprinkling of spinsters who comprised the rest of the congregation, who were receiving the preacher's attention.

"And so my friends, as they cars with them there Londoners and other up-country people go speeding by desecratin' the Sabbath you, wi' their selfish pleasures, let us remember in humility, what a Friend us do have in Jesus. That though us be small in numbers, He baint no ol' counter of heads. . ."

I heard that and felt a twinge of guilt, having ascertained by a count and three re-counts we were twenty-two all told.

"And nor, my friends, is that same Lord Jesus a respecter of age. Here we'm a pretty mixed bag in that quarter—what wi' old Mr. Pengelly back there who I do remember when I was on this circuit thirty or forty year ago—sitting just where he be right now." We all knew where but turned dutifully, nevertheless, to see that ancient white-topped head see-sawing in senility.

"An' then we do have, at th'other end of the scale like, the presence with us of they littluns of whom He did say for us to suffer 'em to go unto Un. . ."

Three rows of heads swivelled back front and up at the preacher, a hard gleam of malevolence in the eyes of our group in the back of the section for being included in the general description of infancy.

"Oh and what delight there be in heaven at the sight of a God-fearing, Jesus-loving youngster."

"Ah go stuff your sel'n," suggested Cousin Jan, before turning his attention once more to the erection in his trousers which he was demonstrating to a trio of fascinated onlookers.

Equally disgusted with the attention of Bonar Law and possibly jealous of Cousin Jan's ability to stiffen virtually at will, I decided this was the moment to liberate the lizard from the empty tobacco tin I had found in the kerb of the highway just after capturing my pet.

For a second or two, as I pressured its tail on the polished pew seat, its tiny feet scratched vainly on the slippery surface. Then a wriggling stump with a bright blob of blood was all I held as a suddenly Manxed lizard slipped over Jan's arm, to stop abruptly on the very pinnacle of his tumescence.

Bonar Law was notoriously hard of hearing but even he could not fail to respond to the loud chortles and guffaws of us older boys and the quick turning round in their pews of the Sunday School classes below us.

"Tis lovely to hear the laughter of youth, my dears, but there's a time and place—"

The lizard swayed as part of Jan jerked. Our commotion increased.

"You gin screw 'un, Jan?"

"Mind you don' open your fly or he'll bite 'un off."

"Make sure he can tell your fly idn' like them he likes," sniggered I the punster.

9

Bonar Law's voice arc'd louder. "Laughter for the 'eathen, for us Methodies 'tis the joy of song. Methodism was born in song me dears, as John Wesley did say when he passed by that very door all them years ago."

"He's going Jan. He's after they other flies on the window sill."

"Grab 'un Harry. I do want 'un back."

"Bidin that harvest is a comin on, let us render to the Lord—We Plough the Fields and Scatter—"

"Our lizard have scattered—ere, this'll scare 'un back." Daniel Tehiddy took my tobacco tin and threw it before I could stop him. It hit Basil Carthew in the row in front who began to cry.

Bonar Law was nigh to shouting: "With joy in our hearts, my friends we shall sing the refrain: 'All good things around us is sent from heaven above.'"

Undone by the excitement of the escaped reptile (or was it uncontrollable lust?) a boy the far side of me (I think it was Jim Trehearne) made a dive at Cousin Jan's possibly already softening member. "Here I know how to get rid of that for 'ee!"

Scuffling broke out, Jan cupping his parts with the speed and precision of years of practice.

"Oh, praise the Lord, Oh, praise the Lord."

Our Aunty Mavis at the harmonium, her angry eyes on us, decided it was time to take the initiative. With a shuffle we all got to our feet. The hymn with its refrain had many stanzas, Aunty Mavis played them all.

By the time we had praised the Lord for all His Love for the umpteenth time, Cousin Jan's erection had subsided completely, the lizard had escaped, and my tobacco tin had been kicked under so many pews that it had long disappeared from sight.

However, endless though the hymn seemed, we sensed that it was not long enough to have driven our activities from the memories of the rest of the congregation.

Bonar Law had scarcely finished bidding the Good Lord good bye on our behalf when the three pew rows of us older boys were making quickly for the exit.

"Let's take the railway embankment," Jan said, "I've

" Zig-Zag " Chapel, St. Kew Highway

Photo : Ray Bishop

Trequite Cross & Hamlet

heard tell there's plenty on they wild strawberries 'long there."

"Yes, let's," I agreed, partly at the thought of the strawberries, but even more at the thought of the lizards that might be basking on the sunny slopes.

We slipped in file across the slate stile nestled between the clumps of hawthorn and alder atop the earth-and-stone hedge. Grasshoppers sprayed before us as they whirred away over the long grass and overhead larks shrilled in the hay-scented air.

Away to our right the galvanized shack of old Jim Polkinghorne stood in its untidy sea of half-husbanded vegetables.

"What about playing up old Jim?" said Jan. "I'd like to hear 'un scream and holler."

"He idn't there," brother Brian piped up in a rare role of news purveyor. "He's into Bodmin. His head started acting up again and they took 'un into the Asylum."

Sure enough there was no thin coil of smoke betokening the preparation of Sunday dinner : Jix, his familiar fawn bitch was not rattling her chain or yapping defiance at us as we crossed the grassfield.

"He 'avn't been in the looney-bin since Christmas," said Jan. "I mind the full moon when Mr. Pasco saw him falling about down to St. Kew ford and picked 'un up and took of 'un in 'isself."

By some unspoken agreement we four boys veered away from the shack.

"Race you to the railway hedge, Jan," I said quickly. And was off through the coarse sedge grass that whipped my bare knees as I ran. Jan was taller than I and far more adept at cutting through the ears that rippled in intermittent waves of fawn and gold as a breeze fingered the fields from off an invisible sea. But in no time, we three flying figures took on the characteristic pattern of our prowess. Lean, tall Jan, a natural athlete, moved swiftly ahead, I ran next, while eleven year old Brian puffed bravely in the rear.

The day seemed to take on an extra ten degrees of heat as we climbed the railway slope, sending clouds of tiny blue butterflies above our toecaps. To the slithering sound of slate dislodged as we clambered up the embankment, we found the frail green leaves of the wild strawberry plants and by deftly following a runner, lifting a leaf, revealed the tiny red orbs against the slate and stone-chipped bed on which they grew. Mysteriously local in their profusion, we would munch happily for seconds on end, silent now in the paradise of wild strawberry taste, before having to move on several yards and discovering another berry trove. Like a small pack of grazing animals on some parched veld we moved slowly along the embankment, imperceptibly climbing higher in our quest.

It was with a jerk of surprise that I lifted my head to see about me the oil-shimmering world of steel rails on a bed of oil-stained stones amid which no grass grew. High, high overhead the inevitable buzzard soared, but in the noon quiet of the summer day there was nothing to disturb the unbroken pall of heat that cellophaned the landscape from the remote rib of Atlantic blue to as far as the questing eye could see.

The others had wandered past me, still picking from the strawberry remnants in their cupped hands. I picked up an oil-streaked granite chip, threw it well over the tops of the trees that screened the lower slopes of the meadows below the embankment the far side from where we had come. Idly watching it disappear in the sun-shot dazzle of the middle air, I looked down to where the grass verge gave out at the edge of the permanent way. Then I tensed with excitement. There, between the raised edge of a dark brown railway sleeper and the shelter of the fringe of grass, basked a lizard. No ordinary lizard, mind, but some ten inches from nose to tail-tip of aqueous green.

Quickly I called to the others, terrified they would turn, approach and send my sun-flattened find scurrying to safety.

" Here—Jan—Brian—wait a mo. I can see a beaut—"

" Where ?"

And more plaintively from Brian, who never saw things first.

" Where's it to, Davey ? "

But attention gained, their movements stopped, I

12

immediately stalked my prey. Jumping down the embankment several yards from where my lizard lay, I approached from below—just in case he should move back and seek the security of the grass.

With a quick check to insure my shadow would not alert him, and getting my hand out well before me so that no hasty movement would be required, I poised my feet, drew breath, and sprang. Right for the head, hoping in the panicked moment he would try and bite my finger and thus, in his puny aggression become my captive. This way no shed-tail defence, no undue crushing of leathery body or fumbling along the squirming length. My aim was as accurate as ever, my technique as successful. With a smile broadening my mouth I returned to my feet, the long green prize wriggling between forefinger and thumb. A small blob of lizard-shit escaped the vent at the joint of the underbelly and tail. Standard attempt on a Sunday walk. Standard result. Only with the sweet rarity of so green, so long, so elegantly tapering a trophy . . .

" Good, you got'n then ?"

" My, he's a heller alright !"

" Proper job, you !"

The praise dizzied my head : my face flushed before I drooped it from their sight. With the return of control I licked lips and looked up.

" I—I think I shall call him Bonar Law," I said.

All Kinds of Harvesting

I looked about me at the stiff-collared navy blue men with their peonie-dressed wives and loved the world. In the circle of farm people, standing outside the Zig-Zag Chapel in the warm dusk of a September evening, a boy belonged.

" Evenin' Harry."

" Evenin' Les."

" A bravun sermon, you."

" Best harvest festival us 'ave had for pretty whiles."

" Well young Davey, standin' there as though butter wouldn' melt in 'ee mouth, be lookin' forward to gin school agin ?"

" Yes, Mr. Hoskyns."

" And you, Jan ? What be a young lad like you looking so sullen for, eh ?"

" Don't know, Mr. Hoskyns."

Honeysuckle scent hung heavily in the air, drowning out the violet and eau-de-cologne smelling ladies with their white court shoes, white gloves that stood out so boldly against the approaches of darkness. I nudged Jan and together we moved away from Mr. Hoskyns and his questions.

" Stupid bugger," said Jan. " One look at un's 'nough to turn anybody's stomach."

Across the road from the small gravel entrance to the chapel, stood a row of tall poplar trees at the gateway of a long drive leading down to a farm : it was there that the younger males congregated after the service, and Jan and I made our way over to where several of our friends stood.

" What be they shits on about then, eh Jan ? Not that stupid preacher dronin' on and on, is it, you ?"

" Dunno," says Jan. " But I can show 'ee what I do think of both he and they."

" What's that, then Jan ?" Jim Trewilliger was always egging on Jan and I hated him for it. It was the side of Jan I didn't care to think about. I knew what he was about to do now and would have turned away if he hadn't been looking directly at me, insisting on my support.

" This boy, this is what they'm worth." He lifted his

right leg off the ground, squeezed his right hand under his left armpit and let out a loud fart.

I laughed with the rest of them, though I secretly called them oafs and wanted to wrinkle my face. From a few yards away I thought I heard Mrs. Pengelly mutter something about filthy creatures and several hostile looks came our way as one boy after the other tried to fart to order as Jan could do so easily.

From out of the trees, one of those sonorous sounding dung beetles zoomed past me, just above my face. The stupid thing ended up by banging against Jim Trewilliger's head and then I really laughed as he yelled against the tiny sting of the impact.

" Serve you right, you maaze indiot," I told myself, " Starting Jan off on all that stuff." (For now Jan was doing a belching act for the rest of them).

Then I saw little Brian detach himself from our parents in the chapel couryard and start across the road towards Jan and me. Even in the weakening light I could see his face looked worried. Perhaps it was my imagination but I suddenly felt a coldness in the air—where a few minutes earlier it had been a balmy September night where grown-ups and we had been held in a bond of peace.

" Davey, Aunt Susan's just asked our mother if Aunt Mat give her Mary's dress after it ud been altered."

" What dress ?" I began, but immediately faltering.

" What dress ? **The** dress, of course ! The one we let Gomer Lane have—he promised us the next lot of white rats from Albert. Back in July month, remember ?"

Thoughts were transcended by a sheer animal rush of feeling — as fear tightened muscles, pricked scalp and broadened my vision. I didn't recognise my voice when it lifted from deep inside. " Jan — look out . . Father . . they know about the dress."

" What dress ?"

" The one we had, fool. Last summer—Mary's."

But already across the lane the adult camp was making ominous manoeuvres. I saw the restraining arm of my mother touch father's sleeve ; saw him brush it brusquely away as he strode forward. Like a detached shadow Jan slipped quietly down the lane. His long length full of grace, he leapt the stile and was then just a dark bobbing head across a patch of shaved corn stalks.

"You'd best be off," Brian said. "You can see what a temper he's in. Look."

"What about you?"

Brian looked up, his grey eyes impassive. "I can't run. I'll hold him up here—if you two get back to the farm first he'll be a bit puffed out anyways. Now go on, Davey."

Hollow-legged, and with an accompanying emptiness inside my stomach awaiting whatever retribution would bring, I slunk off just at the very moment father called out my name.

I began to run where the poplar trees gave out and there was less dusk gathered. Before I followed in Jan's wake, over the stile and across the stubbled field, I saw three figures, now detached from the general group fanning out as they headed in my direction. I suppose if I'd been asked, if someone could have crept into my head and calmed the raging and pounding that went on in there, and asked the identity of the three I might have come up with the names of my father, Uncle Ned and Uncle Joe—brothers all. As it was I saw and felt the devouring pursuit only of three tall men: three figures, black in the dying light, intent on assailing Jan and myself. I knew, every particle of me knew, the power of the Cornish rage, of Celtic tempers from slow-speaking men that could lead to human slaughter on lonely farms, to that moorland obelisk west of Roughtor where, my uncle had told me, a Camelford butcher over a century before had taken his trade to his fiancée in a black passion and hacked girlhood into obscene meat.

No, I did not think of Father and his brothers Ned and Joe. I flamed instead in terror at three giant males who sought only to find our powerless bodies and hammer them till justice for a lost and stolen dress had been shaped from our shrieks of pain.

I cried, moaned rather, into the wind my fleeing shape made as it sped across the squelchy ground. From behind I heard shouts, the angry sounds of retribution, voices calling our names. Ahead, two fields over, I saw the wheatsheaves shacked for carrying; the last field around Pentinny still to

16

be harvested. With the stitch knifing my ribs I ran faster, knowing I could not make the valley's dip of our farm, an outhouse to hide in, or even the familiarity and warmth of my bedroom in which to receive the blows it had been decreed I was to receive.

I reached the five-barred gate leading into the field of shacked wheat, scrambled over it, fell, and leaping to my feet, saw cousin Jan a ghostly outline high on the railway embankment before he darted down the other side. The next second I was tearing at a dew-moistened sheaf and squeezing my body behind it as I strove for the very centre of the corn-stack where, huddled, I would be hid from sight. Welcoming even the dried thistles that needled my back, my legs and hands, thankful for the engulfing blackness as the water from the stalks soaked across my knees, I strove only to keep sound out of the shuddering breaths that shook my whole body before pouring from my gaping mouth.

Then the voices came, faint at first but growing stronger with each breath I took.

"This way, Joe. They young buggers is heading for Tregildern over the railway."

In spite of the dark I closed my eyes ; wrapped scratched hands round drawn up knees to stop their trembling.

"Over this gate. I seen 'un go over'n."

"Gentle Jesus meek and mild, look upon a little child." That was a prayer that mother still made little Brian say before getting into bed. I was too old for it, they told me. But the soft words made me feel smaller in my hiding place.

"Right Ned—this way then."

Then I knew there was no gentle Jesus for me that night. Other god-words pushed at my ears : ' The Lord Thy God is a jealous God,' ' Judgement is Mine Saith The Lord.'

It was a matter of waiting then — of second ticking waiting. I was almost calm when the sheaves were pulled aside and my father's hand crunched at my shoulder and dragged me to my feet.

"There, you little sod, that's for deceit." The stinging slap to my ear didn't quite knock me down.

The blow to the other side of my head did. Father picked me up with one hand, draped me across his knee and began to thrash me.

"This - ul - teach - you - you - young bugger," - his words rhymed with the descent of his hand on my tingling bottom.

Through the yells and sobs of my articulated pain I heard the others.

"Come on then. If us be gin catch young Jan."

"We'll leave 'ee 'ere then, Jack?"

"No you won't." My father let me slide wailing to the ground. "I want that boy mesel.' 'E's th'oldest.. Tis he gin learn I can't abide deceit."

"Twern't jest Jan. Twere all on us," I gulped.

"Git home and git to bed. I want nothin from you, boy cept quiet and out my sight."

I didn't even look up as they made off together, talking in tones as solemn as the punishment they represented.

Muddied, wet but altogether not-caring, I made my way slowly towards our farm. As I dawdled down the final slope of the lane, through the tunnel of giant elms to the faint huddle of whitewashed walls and the precisioned blobs of light from oil-lamp shining windows, there came sounds on the sabbath night that rent the cocoon of pain that had gentled my self-pity from the moment my father's hand had begun to chastise me. As usual in times of inner desolation, I spoke to myself.

"That's it, bully. Hit 'un. Punch and pummel un, you bloody great oaf! Well let I tell 'ee somethin' father - you cas'n hurt 'un. Not deep down you can't. Jan idn' like me. He idn' no coward . . . He idn' no blubberin' weakling."

So sharp a self-evaluation brought tears again to my eyes. Bereft of hope, devoid of self-confidence, and with grief-thickened voice held low against the world in front of me, I asked a sliver of harvest moon, reflected on the duck-pond to my right, why I could not be the person I wished to be.

"Why bain't I got no guts? Why can't I stand up to 'un. Oh why can't I be more like Jan?"

The name of my cousin had no sooner sprung into my head when the squat white door under the jasmine porch suddenly flared with light, and there, running down the path towards the front gate, was Jan himself. A murmur of voices swelled from the front parlour — and died again with a slamming of the front door.

" Jan," I called. " Here. Tis Davey."

The white-shirted figure turned, saw me, and approached slowly, the running somehow all gone out of him.

" What—what did he do, Jan ? Did he . . . did he ?"

" Nothing like what I be gin do to that bastard—you'll see."

" Did—did he hit you, Jan? In front of Uncle Ned and that ?"

" Would've—if ee'd got the chance. I was upstairs in my room. I slipped on the rug as he come in—that's how 'ee was able to hit I when I was down, see. Kept on yelling bout that bloody dress—till I picked up a shoe under the bed and threw un at 'un. Then the bastard really come for I."

" Jan, your lip's bleeding—here, let me see."

" Tis nothin'—I went smack into the bed post. I've broke a tooth too, I think."

" Here, I got a clean hanky. Let's go down by the well."

The tears were back in my eyes. I couldn't help it. For a moment he looked at me. I thought I read uncertainty there.

" Mother and the aunts'll be back soon."

" All right," he said. " Let's go to the well. But no muckin' around, mind. No pretendin' you'm a nurse or any o' that stuff."

" I promise. Tis just that if I can wipe the blood away I can see how big a cut it is."

But with those easy loping strides of his he was already several feet ahead of me going down the steep dip in the hill to the ford where the well was.

As I walked behind him I noticed how he seemed to be breathing more deeply than usual. And his shoulders heaved up and down too. He was more upset, I realized, by what had happened, than anything he had said so far.

It was quite dark down there by the well, but we knew each blade of grass, each sprouting tongue fern by heart. He plonked himself down next to the can we used to scoop the water out of the slate oblong of the well.

" Now come on, bleddy Nurse Nightingale. Let's get this over. I've got to be off."

I poked my finger into the hanky till it made a white worm in the gloom. I stared hard at his tilted face. The red blood looked black as it trickled down to his chin. When the cold of the well water had soaked fully through the hanky to my skin I withdrew it and gently held it to where I thought the cut was. He didn't flinch, but I did. I was glad the night turned the blood black and that the cut was only just visible in the poor light. I could so easily have fainted had all this gone on in the severity of daylight.

" 'Tis quite a deep gash, I think Jan," I said softly. "And there's blood from your nose too."

" I can't feel nothing. Anyway, just wipe it off clean round me chin—then I can get away from here."

I wiped steadily, loving and hating what I was doing.

" Away, Jan ? What you mean ?"

" What I say. Think I'm going to stay roun' here after what that shit said ? Anyway, he told I to get out. Needn't have bothered. I wouldn' spend another night in his stinkin' — "

" Jan—you musn't give in to him. If he **told** you to get out—"

" I thought of it first."

" But Mother wouldn't allow him to send you away—just like that."

" She'd do as he said. She always do, don't she ? Anyway, I'm buggering off. Think I want to see him again after kicking me when I was on the ground ? And all over some stupid bloody dress which I offered to pay for anyway?"

" That must've made him mad. I know he hates it to think you get money from Aunty Jessie."

" Well that's jest where I'm going. To Aunty Jessie's down to Camborne. You finished dabbing me with that thing? "

" That's the mouth done—now for the nose. Don't be impatient Jan. You don't want to look like Dracula, do 'ee ?"

" Wouldn't mind sticking me fangs into his sodding neck."

" Your teeth are too even. You haven't got fangs. Not real ones."

" Well could take a bloody great club then—and smash that down on his skull. That'd do the trick. I tell 'ee, Davey. I hate your father. Hate him."

" Of course you do. So do I. Even Brian doesn't like 'un. But he'll be sorry tomorrow for losing his temper, you'll see."

" No, I won't, 'cause I won't be here."

I cradled his head as I tipped it to stop the water running towards his eyes. " Don't be silly, Jan. That's just playing his game. Here, just let me wring this out. Hold your head just like that."

" You know what he called me ? A thief — and a ungrateful bastard."

Mosquitoes whined about us from the chestnut leaves just above our heads. As I rinsed out the hanky the thought came suddenly, we'd be covered with bites in the morning.

" His names don't count," I said, returning to the task of dabbing his face. " Sticks and stones and all that."

" Not for you maybe. They do for me. Finished ?"

" Nearly. In any case, Jan, you haven't even got your jacket. And you'd need some money."

I felt him relax a little under the support of my arm which was hurting—pushed against a protruding root I think.

" That was what I was gin ask 'ee, I want you to go in and get my coat. Tis over the chair in the back kitchen. And there's some milk money in the jam jar in the dairy. I saw it teatime. One poun' ten . . . "

I didn't answer.

" Well, Davey ?"

I busied myself with his face, even taking the cool handkerchief to his forehead.

" Davey ?"

" Yes ?"

" You haven't answered my question."

" I—I was thinking what it would be like with you gone. Have you thought of that ? Have you thought what they'd do to me if they thought I knew ? Or if I'd helped you go ?" Again those wretched tears blurred my eyes.

There was a silence between us. From a long way away I could hear people's voices. Jan's hand stirred on the mossy ground and I wondered what he was searching for till he found mine and squeezed it. " You can come too," he said. " We can both go. How about that ?"

I stopped dabbing his cut ; screwed up my face as all kinds of things within me wrestled.

" No Jan," I said finally. " Twouldn't work."

The next thing I knew he was on his feet. " You'm a selfish little bugger, Davey—know that? You just want me for your sel'—when it suits 'ee, like."

I jumped up too. " Tidn't true ! I just know that we can't do nothing now. If we go away they'll just bring us back. Later it'll be different. Later they'll have no power over us. Can't you see that ?"

But Jan was already moving away from me, up the other side of the hill beyond the ford. His words came though, quiet but searing, tearing. " You'm just like the rest on 'em. Then you be one of 'em Davey. I was forgettin' that."

" Jan ! Come back. Listen a moment."

But he was too far away to listen, and he never turned again in my direction.

I watched the ghost of his white shirt to the top of the hill, watched it turn and flick from sight. Then, slowly, I turned back towards the opposite slope of the lane and the farm-house beyond. There were no tears now, no hint of them. Just an immense emptiness. As I entered the backdoor I think my father asked me something. Or was it Uncle Ned or Uncle Joe ? I didn't know because my eyes were unseeing, my ears deaf. I went slowly up to bed. Later my mother came up and asked me something in a soft voice. But I did not open my eyes—just feigned the sleep that was all I asked of the world any more.

The next morning Jan appeared at the open dutch door of the back kitchen, his eyes red, hair tousled and his clothes covered with feathers. He had slept the night in a disused fowlshouse in Poltinny meadow, he told me. No one asked him any questions. The dress was never mentioned again.

A First Death

Like the coolest breath, the faintest whisper of upthrust needles in a churchyard yew, the presence of death first brushed my cheek nearly thirty years ago. The time is vivid. So is the place. With scratched red knees, like amulets between sagging navy blue shorts and home-knitted socks whose irregular tops were suspended by silver elastic garters, I wander down the elm gloom of a Cornish lane.

Looking for grass-snakes in the ditch, slashing at stinging nettles with a withy whip, I sang the ditty acquired that morning from a bigger boy in the school playground. With voice more virgin than my thoughts, the peninsular softness of mist permeating my every word, I echoed the information brought to the farms by the alien accents of the B.B.C. and the black banner headlines of the Daily Mail, the Daily Express :

> " Roll along Mussolini, roll along,
> Oh you won't be in Abyssinia very long
> You'll be lying in the grass
> With a bullet up your ass
> Roll along, Mussolini, roll along . . . ."

I liked my voice, took it out for an airing in the private green world of shade that the midges and I dwelt in alone as I climbed, so slowly climbed (my hands pressing on knees for extra strength) towards Tregildern Farm, and the clang of the milking pails as prelude to soft-buttered splits and saffron buns for tea.

> " All glory, laud and honour
> To Thee, Redeemer King —"

Then the vision of chapel morning prison, when Sunday lizards basked in safety from my jam-jar hands, suddenly palled. A quick glance back down the cow-patted wind of the lane, a peering between ivy-fuzzed trunks three times the thickness of me at friendly cows, and a thick-winged buzzard keeping motionless cavey in a patch of blue on behalf of small boys with something to say, though walking alone . . . and I was off.

"Ladies and gentlemen, I have to tell you I've doubled the Air Force, trebled the Navy — and how do you say four times for the Army? It doesn't matter. I don't want to be Prime Minister up this lane anyway."

Save that for Port Quin Cliffs, the shouting over the surf and the dipping, screaming gulls so that the echo bounces back from the packed slate rocks and the whole world knows it's being addressed by a leader of men.

No: for this lane, this Friday afternoon quiet lane, last Saturday's pictures into Wadebridge can be brought out. I would do a Prime Minister before Denis, even before Fred Carhart whom I didn't like but wanted to impress. But this one was only for me. This one I would have died for to save its sound from an alien ear. Quickly I took a grubby grey hanky from my trouser pocket, stuck it over my head, whipped it off again when an invisible shrew rustled and squeaked in anger in the grass-covered hedge, then put it back on, tying two corners under my chin. There was honeysuckle in the air, farmy smells and the acrid whiff of summer-long sun on long-bleached wheat. But not for me there wasn't. I was back in the Saturday cinema, the smell was Jeyes Fluid from the bluish white pools in the open-doored lav at the bottom of the aisles. And from the hushed dark, the soothing projector whirr, there came to clothe me the babushka'd poignancy, the deliciously exotic notes of a mourning mother in an Austrian accent.

Tie the hanky knot just a little tighter — one more glance about for safety. Right now. Hands clenched, face lifted, moistened lips, and eyes to God. Suddenly between the villages of St. Kew and Pendogget in the Cornish heartland Elizabeth Bergner gave the performance of her life in 'Escape Me Never.'

The rabbit-ravaged bank of clay in its lacy festoons of periwinkle and tortured roots became the unfeeling facade of a dismal maternity hospital in a northern industrial city; the sand and granite-chipped ground underfoot, with its lazy

24

trickles of tar, became the steps on which a grief-crazed mother cried . . . .

" Where is my baby?
Where is my leetle baby?
Why haf you taken heem from me?
Please, please give him back to me . . ."

From around the bend a clop of a hoof, the creak of a cart. Quick as a wink the handkerchief's off, the dish-red hands imploring at breasts thrust with hoped-for masculinity into tight trouser pockets. A stone gets a savage kick, is missed, and a spurt of dust must suffice for boy-power as he saunters away from a day in school. It's Mr. Hoskyn with Crippen's moustache from over to Treworden. The little white dog with a black ear and a grass-cutter lameness in the hind leg limps as always under the cart.

" Afternoon Mr. Hoskyn."

" Afternoon boy. Be goin' home then?" (Silly ol' bugger — where the hell do he think I be going?)

" Yes, I reckon. Tis bravun hot you, bain't it?"

" Better than wishy weather boy—no cause to grumble, you. Whoa there, Ruby. Godammee, hoss, you'm like a bleddy colt when 'tidn' necessary — an' fit for the knacker's yard when I do want a bit a sweat out on 'ee."

" Reckon I best get on, then, Mr. Hoskyn. I bide Father will have I help wi' milkin'. They'm still carryin' down to Pol'garrow. He'll be short-handed."

" Bain't your dad 'ull be wantin' of 'ee. Tis your mother. Her's over to your Great Aunt Sarah's, I heard tell up village. She've took a turn for the worse, you. Poor old soul! 'Tidn' no surprise, mind. Why, 'twere maze on her be working up field so long as she did — her goin' on ninety."

" I'd best hurry then. Thank 'ee Mr. Hoskyn . . . "

But the words were already mechanical, the horse and cart, the red face under the bandless panama already blotted black in a sea of widow's weeds. Great Aunt Sarah . . . . widowed by war . . . . two sepiaed sons curling on a mantelpiece who'd ploughed the Somme, someone (my brother?) had told me, with dum-dums in their tum-tums. The church-smelling room with twin beds, dried out Woodbines in a sunbrowned package, waiting for the last trump to get smoked. Shoes polished and neat under the beds. Young men's suits (yes, it was definitely my brother who told me) hung in the great walnut wardrobe askew on the uneven floor.

Back to the black of widow's weeds . . . old ladies smell of lavender, I read in a library book. Not my great aunt. She had no smell. Feel she had. But no smell. Small tight cheeks, high up and almost too close to the currant eyes. There it was safe though. Hard but safe. For kissing I mean. Below, towards the chin, towards the mouth was a stifling blanket. If you missed when you reached up to give that demanded peck you got the place where it all caved in, where you felt if you weren't careful, your lips would sink and sink until your nose was involved too and soon you'd suffocate — halfway through to the back of her head. The softness was the worst of her though. Apart from that everything was interesting. Sometimes a little frightening, but always interesting. Her arms and body, for instance. Hard, brittle hard, for the flesh had long since melted and dripped from her bones. Her gums were as good as teeth. They could easily break and crumble those great square hard-tack biscuits (dog biscuits we called them) that, along with orange peel and bananas, seemed to provide her sole sustenance.

Boy's lace-up boots on her ankle sticks, black from there on to the scrawny wattle of her neck. Her hair, white what there was, but that only wisps and tufts nervously peeping from under the flattening weight of her eternal, lacquer-black bonnet.

As I hurried I grew nervous. There were other things. The plunge into her softness beneath the cheekbone was unpleasant, but it was something known, something to plan against. But what of the unknown things, without shape, without any form to roll about in my mind till safe with familiarity? Down below . . . between her legs. What was there at ninety? My brother, Brian, told me that she was too old to need anything to drink and that meant she didn't

26

piddle any more either. All right, women were pretty nothing in front anyway. And if no water and all dried up — well, I could always make my nose wrinkle like a rabbit's by thinking about things like that. But I could always dance my mind away if from just nose-wrinkling I started to feel hot round my neck.

But there was something else. Up her front, somewhere above her invisible wrinkled waist, I knew there was something horrible. I'd read it in the Scriptures, heard it from the pulpit (not in Church but in Methodist Chapel when Fisherman Trehearne from Port Isaac got carried away over the Witch of Endor). Deep from sight, hidden since before husband and sons went and stayed on the Somme, were what I knew to be called withered dugs.

I left the lane at Pentire Turn, the Primitive Methodist Chapel peeked a fretwork gable from behind a haystack. And I thought of the withered dugs and trembled . . . No need to tell me what a dug was like ! The clue was in the sound. A dug was a slug, a slimy slug living of that dried withered old skin in that awful darkness under her layers and layers of widow's weeds. Blind like a mole, a nude not a velvet mole, those white and wizened suckers parasited in hideous quiet. I never kissed her front on, terrified of feeling movements from the dugs clinging to her dried-out breasts. But always quickly, from the side.

Then that summer, just as Mussolini rolled and rolled, she had taken to her bed. Old Doctor Menhennit from Camelford visited her, mother, Cousin Vin, and Second Cousin Matthilda visited. But I didn't. What — what if I should go there when the clothes were up? The darkness banished and the oil-lamp light showing the dugs asleep on the yellow wax of her flesh?

I was hurrying now. Past the squat granite grin of old Mr. Pengelly's cottage with its wisteria eyebrows, past the rust-red village pump with the faint stench of bad eggs from the previous week when my brother, Brian, and my cousin, Ted, had fought with the spoils of a deserted nest from the White Wyandottes on Tremain's farm.

Why am I hurrying? To see? To have obscenity unpeeled and lay bare the unholy secrets of old-woman age?

No. I hurry because I am cloaked now in guilt. Since St. James' Day, when no black draped dwarf had huddled on the vicarage lawn for the church fete, or limped elmward with ashplant stick to escape the sudden July rain, I had turned away.

"Davey, Great Aunt Sarah's feeling poorly, will 'ee come over with I dear? There's a good boy?"

"Mother — I told 'ee this morning I promised to take Fennel's yeast off the Southern National down to 'em."

"Great Aunt was very good to your Daddy and I when we was first married, and her've loved you boys ever since you were tiny tackers — won't 'ee visit her after chapel Sunday? She asked for 'ee special Davey, when only Brian went over afore."

"I'm feeling poorly too, Mother. My head is proper aching."

"She's got a bar of that there Cadbury's for 'ee — bought it special. There idn' a reason from Genesis to Revelation why 'ee don't drop by for a visit. I bide 'twould do her the world of good."

"I be going, mother — I tol' 'ee, darnee, I be goin'. Only next week."

That was this week — roll along Mussolini, roll along week.

'That's a car outside her place. Old blue Ford. That belongs to the Vicar. Her's always chapel though — 'cept for St. James' Day. That's my bike. Tis Brian, the bloody heller! Why can't he take his own? Just cause mine's newer! Half the village's here if you ask I . . . '

"C'mon in dear. Mother's in there with your Great Auntie."

"Tis a sad day to Pendoggett. Us bain't gin see the likes on her agin."

"Mother? They said as how you was here."

"Shshsh!"

"I — I met Mr. Hoskyn. How . . . how is she?"

"Her've gone, Davey — less than an hour 'twas. Her was here for pretty whiles though. Her've no regrets I reckon."

Slowly tentatively, I looked up the heavy white coverlet

and saw her half-crowned, chinstrapped death. Under the coins her eyelids slept, the ribbon about her head returned to her the jutting chin I had never known yet which she was to bequeath to me and mine. I did not think of the dugs. I sniffed for the smell they had told me of but she betrayed no more in death than in life.

"You may kiss her dear. I bide now's the time. Th' others is coming."

Leaning over, my lips tipped the shiny blue veined dome and I thought — 'She looks funny without her hat.' I blinked my eyes to share the moist faces of those standing quietly around, but nothing came.

Finally bored when excluded from adult tears, I slipped away and over to the cowshed under the granary. As I squeezed the dappled tits of the big roan Ayrshire I tried hard again, even screwing up my eyes and thinking of Jesus on the Cross to make something of ashen Great Aunt Sarah. But nothing would come.

Mussolini rolled on and away into the damp of Autumn. A rainy dusk after evensong. In my pocket was a squirming bat, lifted from the porch rafters with an umbrella borrowed from the worm-holed stocks skirting the slate-flagged floor, while its owner delayed in the oil-lamp light of the Norman church.

Hurrying ahead of the congregation, I dodged down the years and centuries of my turf-covered kin, till screened from sight by a trio of young yews. About to bring forth my palpitating bat, I glanced at the granite headstone on which I leant. 'Sarah Bassett Nankivel, aged 91 years. Beloved wife,' etc . . . I thought of her, back one already fading summer. Munching her crumbly biscuit she had brought a pasty out of the large straw basket she was carrying :

"Here, my dears. Half for 'ee, Brian — and half for 'ee, Davey. And there bain't so many as knows how to bake a pasty so 'twould break even enough for Solomon hisself!"

The widow's weeds went, and there was only the spit of rain in the rising wind. The river below the dead gurgled. Over in Mr. Bailey's byre a cow lowed quietly to its calf.

My fingers gently encircled the warm and furry body of my bat for comfort.

Rosemary

Down through the yellow years I glimpse the billowing hem of your dress as it blends then breaks free from the dancing white of the hawthorn blossom. When the earth cracked with the rush of Spring and we—you, Rosemary, me and my cousin Jan—lay on the young green grass, watched only by skylarks as we fumbled with bud-hands to unfurl our puritan leaves.

Of me, of course, you will have no memory. It was brown and lissome Jan, whose shock of black hair fronded your cheeks as he lay astride you on the warming earth, who laughed his breath in yours.

I, little and sick with fear, pushed my bewildering stiffness down between the clumps of sheep-shorn turf—and watched from a remote country two adolescent bodies squirming, wrestling, to find the rhythm of an April day . . .

I saw garments known only before as white dancers on a wind-gusted clothes line strung across a mowey fall, like petals, as you arched your back. And as you rose with his rhythm for the very last time, sighed and grew quiet, I sensed that innocence had taken you to the place where you and he had sought so blindly for so long.

But the whiteness flickers in the stain of green grass : the mood changes with the setting sun. From the elm-clad slopes, the churchtower-perforated hills, between the exhilarating moor and the swirl of the Atlantic, curls the rancid steam of rural gossip.

" Have 'ee heard tell, you, that Rosemary over to Trehearne bain't nothin but a shameless huzzy ?"

" Yes, my dear, you may flash they teeth as you do cycle by wi' all they ' good mornin's ' and ' good evenin's ' but tis on your back wi' legs akimbo you be spendin' half your hours."

" Have 'ee heard, boy ? Ol' Rosemary up to Treherne will let any on us screw her ! Jim Pengelly 'uv had her . . . An' Harry Hoskyns, an' Ben Nankivel."

" My Dad says how she'm a whore—'ow all them Bryants be so."

" My Grandad did tell I 'ow ol' Petherick Bryant did hide away in Broodymoore woods for the whole of the Great War. 'Fraid they was gin take 'un to fight they Germans. I would'n' want to touch no maid wi' that kind of blood, I don' mind a tellin of 'ee."

" 'Er was seen to Tregildern—up in the cornmow, laughin and carryin on with Danny Carhart."

" Eez—and the same weekend, you, her was to pictures down 'Bridge with one o' they Trethews from up Pendoggett."

And so the talk grew. Laughing smut-sprayed talk in playgrounds, on the train from Camelford with the high school set. Muttered with vicious earnestness on the green National bus by bun-haired matrons on market day. As steel-pronged forks flashed in the evening sun atop rising hay-stacks, from tobacco stained teeth came the soft-burred sounds that turned poor Rosemary's whiteness grey.

Until it reached the white-cob walls of the farmhouse where Jan and I dwelt. A Saturday night in late July, fresh from the galvanized bath with its watery freize on the slate floor before the kitchen range, we boys sat in dressing-gowned warmth listening to the accumulator-fresh sounds of Variety from the wireless set in the deep recess of the front kitchen window. Mother was baking pasties and pies, father talking outside in the dusk by the barn door. We sat at the shiny oak table, a habit from the homework nights of winter, listened to Florence Desmond, Gert and Daisie and Claud Dampier's troubles with his landlady. But all the time, between our laughs, between our mind's travels to an unknown London in an unknown England, we listened also to the steady drone of the two farmers in the bat and barn-owl gloom beyond the fuschia hedge.

Ours was a strict house : at nine o'clock with the Big Ben gong from behind the lattice of wooden tulips and the dimly answering Westminster chimes from the mantelpiece in the Sunday-awaiting musty parlour, we boys would be bustled bedward.

This night, though, was different. The man out there, propped on his bike, anticipating the sabbath in his blue serge suit and with shoes rather than boots beneath his bicycle-clip ankles, was Rosemary Bryant's father. Trehearne farm lay the far side of Polgy-Wurgy woods ; what was more, the Cornish Arms lay a half mile further away still and this was Saturday night . . . A premonition had stirred in me like a restless breeze when I had peered over the open half of the sash window and seen that tall figure walking up the steep hill from the ford.

What had brought him along the rough road from Trequite ? The lane that bifurcated our farm led only to the Red Lion (which the Bryants never used) and then the Turnpike and the Primitive Methodist Chapel. And the Bryants were Church.

Jack Warner finished minding his bike ; a deep throated Denis Noble began to sing of Drake's Drum ; the break was ideal.

" Jan ?"

" What do 'ee want ?"

" Know who that is ? Out there talking wi father ?"

" No." Jan was not a talker.

" Tis Mr. Bryant—Rosemary's father."

" So ?"

" He isn't out there for nothing. Why idn' 'ee down to The Cornish Arms ? that's where all the Pencarrow people go Saturdays."

" How should I knaw ?"

" I was watching 'em while you was emptying the bath. They looked pretty serious — kept on looking in here. I reckon tis about Rosemary."

" What about Rosemary ?"

" I—well, I was thinking of that time . . ."

" What time ?"

" You know—when you and her—out in the meadow beyond the mowey ?"

" When I 'llowed you to watch ?"

In the pause a moth fluttered heavily towards the white incandescence of the hanging lamp's mantle. The wireless oscillated faintly.

" Yes."

" There've been others since then for her—why pick on me ?"

" You was the first, Jan. You said she told 'ee that."

The exchange lapsed to the crunch of feet on the gravel path. I felt my sweat and prayed for another comedian to follow Denis Noble. My father never, never used that front path . . .

I began to cry before Jan's name was thundered from the suddenly incongruous jasmine porch, and remember the hefty slap around the face from my father's hairy, milk-smelling hand as he charged past, sending chairs flying as he grabbed out and missed the retreating figure of his nephew who was already making for the stairs.

White faced and trembling I huddled on the couch as far from the light of the lamp as I could get, while above the crashes and thuds bulged the boards of the kitchen ceiling and sent a host of dust motes into the air above me. As Mother screamed and Father shouted, as Jan cursed them both for the death of his mother, Alvar Liddell told me and a great yellow moth, of battleships sunk and of bombs on cities.

The North country twang of J. B. Priestley jollied along about English decency while I felt the trickle of diarrhoea and rocketed heavenward prayers for dear Jan and the destruction of my father.

Of the rest of that day I now see only a small, slope-ceilinged room with wallpapered rafters prominent from the uneven walls, a floral designed bowl and pitcher on the washstand — and the naked candle on the commode we were forbidden to use . . .

I remember feelings though — and a handful of sounds. From outside in the farmyard Skipper barked, and rattled the chain from his kennel, the rats in the cornbin squeaked as always and, as the farm gathered in quiet, there came the sibilant hiss of my father pissing over by the damson tree before turning in for the night.

There may too, have been a little sob from me when I crept in beside Jan and he whispered " Silly little bugger — they can't hurt me." . . .

Once more, Rosemary, did you flit into the motley of softening, slipping images that belonged to my last years in the farmland of my shaping. And that too stands in the strength of its association with whiteness : your whiteness . . .

34

A Lane in St. Kew Parish

Photo : Ray Bishop

North Cornish Landscape

Photo : Ray Bishop

The period was still one of National Dried Milk and powdered eggs, of ersatz saffron for the Cornish, of personal points for sweets, dockets for utility furniture and coupons for virtually everything else. The war, though, was over - won, they said . . .

The granite-walled grammar school above one railway station, to which I walked each school morning for six years across the bowl of Bodmin, cradled on the edge of the moor from the other station, had now done with me. Staying with father's first cousins in palm-treed Falmouth I attended art school, wore a long scarf and smoked a large pipe stuck incongruously in the centre of a too rose-budded mouth.

Falmouth meant ships, and ships sliding in and out of the broad but unhurried harbour spelt that other Cornwall of abstracted exile. Wherever, in fact, men with the skills of Camborne and Redruth, in their bones, had gone in successive generations as Cornish moles to dive once more under the earth's crust in an alien place for the copper, silver and tin, lead and antimony, they had mined on their ancient peninsular since at least the days of Alexander the Great.

But away from the cob-walled womb of Lanharrow was as easily sixty thousand miles as sixty for me at eighteen. Already the melancholy of diaspora seized me, though I had not as yet succumbed to the Celtic westward trek.

When classes ceased for the Easter break I hurried home to North Cornwall, hitch-hiking my way between the heights of heather-fringed granite and the warm, equally un-English valleys where tamarisk jostled with seas of creeper.

When I arrived, though, it was to find such heart-stirring landmarks as the snaking Camel, estuarying its way past Padstow, the clump of clay pyramids towards St. Austell, and the moony surface of the moor itself, all somewhat intimidated by a sequence of hard blue days with hoar frost lingering late.

The crispness of morning, which seemed to be holding both hedgeflowers and birdsong at bay, tingled my ear lobes as I sped about the villages with straw frails * of bottled milk from our farm suspended from cold handlebars. Instead of charging my spirits behind wind-watered eyes, the nip in

* frails = baskets made of raffia in straw

the air somehow numbed me. (Too many months in the decadent balm of Falmouth?) As I dropped my bike and walked to council house and cottage backdoors I began to hope that Mrs. This and Mrs. That would not be frying up breakfast and thus see me as they sent bacon smells across back gardens.

But it was not to be. They saw me, knew me to be back from Cousin Kate's down to Falmouth, and wanted therefore to talk. These were the regulars, those whose hair-curlered heads I had seen above kettle steam and sizzling frying-pans since I had first pushed the milk bike, then a giant, when I was twelve.

There was Mrs. Trethewey on the second morning. Missing my absent cousin, now away at agricultural college, I had moped the previous unseasonably cold day by the open-grated kitchener, answering mother with mono-syllables as she questioned me over the art school and my cousin's menage while I felt lonely and superior in a new vocabulary of art, a new slang amid student friends.

Mrs. Trethewey neither knew nor cared of any such things.

" Morning Mrs. Trethewey."

" Morning Boy. Back then from down there."

" Just for the holidays."

" They devils got 'ee back to the milk round soon enough, 'aven't em?"

" They're still short-handed. What with Basil not demobbed yet."

" I reckon. Bet Mother's tongue be just as sharp as when 'ee left, you, eh? Better up on that bike than 'earing of her moan 'fore breakfast."

" She do complain too much, though we've told her enough times. Will it be one skim milk this morning then, Mrs. Trethewey?"

" She do want everybody else to be doin' too much, you, that's 'er trouble. I always tell our Fred to send a pint of bitter over to your Dad when he comes into the Inn. One skim and one ordinary. And you tell her the bill was wrong. I paid two Fridays ago—not dree."

36

" I'll tell her. There we are then. Best be moving on I 'spose."

" I reckon as how you and Jan b'aint heard her yap for years. Closed off your ears you did. Don't blame 'ee neither. Coming Fred—impatient begger. See him with tea an no milk in't! I'm tellun 'ee!"

" Morning Mrs. Trethewey."

" Morning Boy."

At Mrs. Trevethen's the exchange on the tiny slate-floored porch took on an even more personal note.

" You'm back then. Save your father a mile or two in the morning's eh ?"

" Yes, I reckon. Pint and a half, isn't it, Mrs. Trevethen?"

" Eees. Damnee, you've grown, boy bain't ee ?"

" Have I ?"

" Here, bet you do know what tis for wi' they Falmouth maids, eh? Learnt to use 'un proper, ave 'ee? No more that playin wi' 'ee self to Broody-moor woods from now on, eh Boy ?"

" Ah, Mrs. Trevethen !"

" Darnee if I bain't embarrassin of 'un ! Can 'ee still blush then ? Here, let's 'ave a look." She'd been asking the length of it for years, that dirty old woman. I stepped back quickly.

" What's the matter then? 'Fraid I be gin pull it off 'ee, that it ?"

" It's just the milk-round, I got a lot more to deliver yet."

" I bet 'ee 'ave. And not for the likes of me, you ! Well I'm glad to see you be catching up to that Jan. Time you was developing a bit, boy. " I mind the time when your Father—"

" Goodbye Mrs. Trevethen." I fled, to her raucous laughter shattering the peace of the early morning valley.

The third of my milk-round harpies, perhaps through some diabolical telepathy, took up where Mrs. Trevethen left off.

Mrs. Sanderstead was there, waiting as I trudged the cindered path from the outhouse where I propped the bike.

" If it idn' your father all over again ! Why if you'm half the heller he was you won't find me 'ere in me dressing gown no more. Tis a proper young stallion you'm turned into Davey."

"Thank you, Mrs. Sanderstead. A pint for you and a pint for your daughter-in-law, I think Mother said."

"Said ? Screamed at 'ee I reckon ! Tis proper bedlam round there at this time of day, bain't it ? That's why your ol' man likes to get out with the milk. That an' other things . . ."

"I'm just here for the holiday. Just three weeks. Hope the weather warms up at that."

"You do—and the maids too if they do get a look on 'ee. Scamperin' like mice they'll be when they smell the sap runnin high in 'ee."

"Well, I best be off, now. Morning Missus."

"Morning, Boy. Just a half tomorrow, mind."

The only difference between all this and all the frosty mornings of my childhood milk-round chore, was my failure to respond in kind. Before my voice broke I had told Mrs. Sanderstead she should talk less and get Les Sanderstead to do more. Once hairpinned Mrs. Trethewey had thrown a cat's saucer at me when, from the safety of my bike, I said I was saving up for better than the likes of her Mary. But on the eve of my eighteenth birthday, in spite of the armour of pipe and scarf, the heady language of Impressionism and Realism, I felt sad at my Easter home-coming ; sad and desolate. Jan was gone. The farm was no longer home in quite the same way. And nobody, in the village or in the house, was as interested in my Falmouth exploits as I had expected them to be.

With milk-round done, sticks chopped, and log-sawing for the great washing copper in the linney completed, I took to wandering the fields alone, half-wishing I had brought a friend home from art school as Mother had suggested in a letter, but half-content with the self-pity and moody dreams that swam so easily amid my cast-down spirits.

Until one morning after the bells of the valley had clanged out Easter I found myself crossing the stepping stones of the ford and clambering up the churchyard slope, where the cawing rooks wheeled overhead and the chiselled names of my family gently dissolved above untidy grass mounds. Self-conscious, wanting to be romantic, thinking of sad young poets and how much sweeter was the sleep of death than the rude prod of life, I suddenly looked in the direction of the church on hearing the murmur of voices. I was in time to see Mrs. Trevethen and Mrs. Sanderstead entering the porch together. Behind them were a scattering of others . . all women . . all familiar to me as from our village.

I sauntered forward, lingering though, about the last frieze of tombstones, until it looked as if all the matrons of Pentinny had been gathered into the dim and dank smelling quiet of our Norman church.

Just about to pass under the sundial and by the Elizabethan stocks ranged on each side of the church porch, I heard a further crunching of gravel behind me and a mutter of restrained voices. There, just turning the bend, in a sea of gossamer white as she clutched the navy-blue arm of her father, was Rosemary. Lace floating prettily about her dark face, a satin train slipped cleverly over her free arm as her dainty white feet sped the yellow gravel, she looked as radiant as the newspapers always said brides did.

Terrified of encountering her, retreat cut off by the wedding party's approach, I hurried in on the wake of our milk-round customers.

I took the back pew and the furthest corner. The women sat towards the front but scattered in pairs and trios across two aisles. For want of better to do I counted a dozen bodies other than my own. In the very first pew stood the tall figure of a man in airforce blue. He glanced round nervously. His was the only unfamiliar face.

Behind me the sexton's gnarled hand started pumping the protruding wooden shaft of the organ blower and quickly the creaking mechanism drowned out his own wheezing. With bent back and a sliding, crab-like shuffle, Mr. Trewin, our Vicar, hurried in magpie robes past my pew towards the candlelit sanctuary. A burst of music discordantly, jaggedly, played by Miss Treece from the almshouses, and Rosemary's white-clouded self sailed down the aisle to where groom and priest awaited her.

After the customary drawn-out wheeze of the organ when the music had died down, Mr. Trewin began . . .

" Dearly beloved, we are gathered together here in the sight of God, and in the face of this company, to join together this man and this woman in holy matrimony ; which is an honourable estate, instituted of God, signifying . . . unto us . . . ''

But the dearly beloved gathered there together in the sight of God had already begun to talk.

From Mrs. Sanderstead a stage whisper.

" Look on her. Shameless huzzy ! Wearin' white indeed !''

" Signifying unto us the mystical union that is betwixt Christ and his church : which holy estate . . . ''

Mrs. Trethewey from two pews over was not to be out-done by Mrs. Sanderstead.

" Her've forgotten what 'twas to be a virgin. On her back for seven summers. Why black itself's too white for the likes on her.''

Mr. Trewin droned on. " Into this holy estate these two persons present come now to be joined. If any man can show just cause why they may not lawfully be joined to-gether, let him now speak, or else hereafter for ever hold his peace.''

But these were women who intended to speak if for no other reason than that they were quite incapable of holding their peace for God or man.

" Look at that poor bugger. If tis her maidenhead 'ee be after 'es got a bravun long hunt.''

" Reckon as how he were the only one up to Davidstow airdrome that could'n get away then?''

" 'Tis her father I be sorry for—Mind you, he's no better than he need to be.''

" I require and charge you both . . . if either of you know any impediment, why ye may not be lawfully joined together in Matrimony, ye do now confess it.''

" Young Binnegar to St. Tudy had her when they was both still tiny tackers. Our Fred seen 'em at it.''

" White weddin indeed ! Even our Mary didn' have nerve enough for that !''

(Then from the bridal group :)
" Be quiet !"
" Quiet your sel'n !"
" Norman, wilt thou have this woman . ."
" Let him 'ave 'er—everybody else 'ave!"
" Shsshsh !"
" Wilt thou love her . . ."
" Jest like all the young stallions round here 'ave !"
" I am afraid I must ask for quiet in the nave." Old Trewin looked venomously over glasses at his unruly congregation.

" Registry office would 've thrown her out, I don't doubt."
" Hold your tongue, woman."
" Rosemary, wilt thou have this man to thy wedded husband ?"
" Like 'twould make a change for 'ee my dear ?"
" Shshsh !"

We never did hear either Norman's or poor Rosemary's assent. At breakneck speed the Vicar charged through the service, to the continuing debate between the wedding party and Pentinny's free-speaking ladies.

Jumping whole collects, prayers and admonitions the Vicar took refuge in the Blessing.

" God the Father, God the Son, God the Holy Ghost, bless preserve and keep you."

Mrs. Trethewey, famous for her last words, managed a parting shot.

" Ess, my dear, and you do need all the Trinity and more to keep her from sniffin' round other men."

Miss Treece, long since straining at the leash, or rather the organ console, plunged in then with her own esoteric version of ' The Voice That Breathed O'er Eden.' Before Mr. Trewin's hand had descended from Benediction, the Pentinny chorus of revolt had upped and begun to flee the church. Before an approximation of Mendelssohn had usurped the last stanza of the hymn, I decided to make myself scarce too.

Blinking out in the fitful sunlight now crumbling the leaden day, I stood over by Great Aunt Sarah's mound to watch the bride and groom emerge. The ladies from the council houses and nearby cottages stood in a straggling line along the edge of the path. Their hands were raised for the traditional throwing of confetti and I had time to wonder at their abrupt change of heart.

As Rosemary in her billowing cloud came forth with her airman at her side, there was a cheer from the strung out onlookers. Ironic perhaps? I couldn't be sure. Not until, that is, the confetti began to be cheerfully hurled at the approaching party. I saw one or two bits of paper floating down through the air, but before that I heard the grit splatter against the slate headstones—and realized where the confetti had come from.

Those ladies had picked the remnants from the last wedding off the path they stood on. Not surprisingly they collected more grit than paper. As the couple broke into an undignified trot—(to escape the stinging hail of minute granite chips) — I had one last glimpse of my snow-white dream. Of a tear-puffed face and an askew veil.

I ducked quickly out of sight as Rosemary's parents appeared, with Mr. Trewin in their wake. Still the ladies were bending, scooping, lifting and throwing, as the assembly were finally cut off from my view. One particularly noisy shout came to me, followed by an angry slamming of a car door.

I have never seen you, Rosemary, from that day to this. Nor, I think, has Pentinny. Jan told me, just before his own wedding to a Plymouth nurse, that you now lived in Calgary. You were quite happy, he said, and the mother of an eight pound baby boy you had called Jan.

First Job

I sat and stared gloomily out of the newspaper office window at poplar trees and the parish church opposite. I was seventeen and it was my first day of work, and I was depressed at the ubiquity of old men. It was the tail-end of World War Two, and I had only really got the newspaper job because the hale and hearty were away fighting it.

So I was landed with Mr. Trebilcock and Mr. Tremayne. Mr. Trebilcock wore funny old-fashioned collars, was terribly thin and had long, dandruffy hair that made him look like a scruffy Franz List from the back. Mr. Tremayne, on the other hand, had quick, darting movements, was plump, and had black, fieldmouse eyes and a lobster pallor that presaged the heart attack which was to fell him a few months later.

But it was the combination of the work and Mr. Trebilcock that depressed me most. He reeked the cancer that had been assigned to him - only I was ignorant of illness and had little sense of a man's mortality. All I saw, sitting opposite me at that huge table, with its copy-spikes, its litter of galley-proofs, and ashtrays piled with the ugly butts of hand-rolled cigarettes, was that sunken face with its dew-drop eagle nose and that foul-looking fag stuck to the upper lip right under it.

Mr. Trebilcock held the galley and poised his precisely-sharpened pencil to make corrections. My job was to read the copy aloud - a task which he synchronized with a silent moving of those bloodless lips as his eyes blearily sped along the printed lines of the galley proofs.

" . . . . . the bride was attired in a navy blue suit with white accessories. They will honeymoon in Penzance . . Pleading guilty, 23-year old Ivor Pendorrick asked for thirty other cases to be taken into account . . . . "

" Count or account ?"

" Account, Mr. Trebilcock."

" Speak up, son. No good mumbling in this business."

" No, Mr. Trebilcock."

" And stop calling me Mr. Trebilcock. Takes too long."

" What shall I call you then? "

43

" Sir."

" Oh come, Trebilcock! This is 1945, not 1900. You just use what title comes naturally, Davey."

" Yes, Mr. Tremayne."

Tremayne sat at the other end of the room from us. He was boss, and I guess old Trebilcock resented being brought back from retirement to serve under someone several years younger and who, in the old days, had been his junior.

" Well, let's get on with it," Trebilcock grumped. " Be here all night otherwise."

" Opening the fete at St. Merryn, the Vicar, the Rev. A. C. Trewin, welcomed representatives of both the Fleet Air Arm and a R.A.F. contingent from St. Eval . . ."

I faltered.

" Whassa matter? " Trebilcock mumbled.

" I don't think it's Trewin at St. Merryn. The Rev. Pocock's down there."

" Good boy! Good boy! " said Tremayne, his fat face wreathed in smiles of encouragement. " That's the first thing about working on a local paper, my lad — to have local facts at your fingertips. Upcountry newspapers got nothing to teach us 'bout that!"

" Well, at least the Western Morning News taught me what a deadline was," my colleague directly across from me spat acidly. " Cause in they days we weren't running a kindergarten, you !"

" I'm sorry, Mr. Trebilcock," I said, putting all the politeness I could muster into it. " I'm sorry I'm so young. I'll try and do something about it."

For a second those watery eyes lifted and surveyed me. Wondering whether I'd really given him lip or not, I thought as I stared back impassively. Then he must have thought better of it. I watched him strike out Reverend Trewin's name and substitute that of Pocock. When he'd done it I started reading again.

" . . . . . Mrs. Hannah Hawkey, of Nankivell, will again represent the Women's Institute at the Royal Albert Hall in London . . . ."

Mr. Tremayne got up, beamed, and made for the door.

"Back in a jiffy," he said, before disappearing.

"Jiffy — hell!" sniffed Trebilcock. "Won't see him back before lunchtime, I'll tell you that!"

It wasn't something I felt capable of commenting on, so I held my peace. Or rather, I continued reading copy.

". . . . Trapped for several hours in a bog on Bodmin Moor, a heifer belonging to R. J. Bray, of Bolventor . . . "

But Mr. Trebilcock was obviously tired of correcting galleys. "Oh shut up!" he said, dropping the folded bundle of proofs on the table before him and puffing on his mottled cigarette. "If he can slip out for a drink and place his day's bets, we can at least rest up from reading about bloody bullocks and the like."

I found the vision sparked by Trebilcock of Mr. Tremayne drinking and gambling his way through the middle of the morning an intriguing one.

"Where . . . where does Mr. Tremayne do his . . . go for a drink then?"

"He bain't particular. Conservative and Unionist Club . . . The Cornish Arms or the Red Lion. It's all the same to him. The club's for the betting though — he can only booze in the pubs."

I waited expectantly. To hear one old man being disloyal about another was a novel experience. Then I decided to egg old Trebilcock on. It was certainly better than reading proofs for hours on end.

"You're not a drinking man yourself then, Mr. Trebilcock?"

"In working hours? Certainly not, my son. Then of course I'm from Launceston — not a drunken hole like this."

I didn't know Launceston very well, but from what I remembered it wasn't that different. Maybe a few less pubs and fish-and-chip shops. So what? However, after some two hours' acquaintance I'd already learned with Mr. Trebilcock that it didn't do to flatly contradict him.

"Launceston's better then, is it?" I asked conversationally. "I don't really know it."

"Better? Well, when I was your age I wouldn't have had to ask that — 'cause they still gave us in school what was then correctly called an education."

He sat back, re-lit his scruffy cigarette — which kept going out, I noticed — and addressed some spot above my head and behind it. Probably that long Georgian sash window, or the churchyard and its line of poplar trees.

"A town is more than a pile of buildings, you know. It's worth its vision of itself."

"I see," I said.

He wholly ignored that. "Launceston, as you'd know if you'd ever done any history, was the ancient capital of Cornwall. It's much older than a place like this. Altogether a more, well, sophisticated place."

"I see," I repeated.

"You see too bloody much," he commented drily. "What you need more of is hearing. Listen to your elders a bit more — that's my advice to you, my son."

I could have done without his advice — just as I could have done without that spray from his thin lips which kept coming closer and closer to me across that polished expanse of table.

"I hear," I said, looking him straight in the face. "I hear you very well, Mr. Trebilcock."

(Inside my head, of course, my words formed somewhat differently: Hell to you, Mister Tre-bloody-bilcock! Why don't you bugger off to the churchyard, eh? 'Cause that's where you belong by the looks on 'ee).

"You've certainly got enough lip for an ignorant little runt," my elderly colleague informed me. "Then I 'spose the world they're fighting for over there is going to be for the likes on you. Thank God I shan't have no part on it, though. That's what I say!"

"You don't approve of democracy, Mr. Trebilcock? Or maybe — " Then I stopped. I knew that I was moving fast from giving him a bit of cheek to just trading insults.

"I suppose life had its points in olden times too, eh, Mr. Trebilcock? It's just that I wouldn't have liked to go to work sweeping chimneys as a kid of six or seven. And all that unemployment before the war — I reckon I wouldn't 've cared for that either."

"Kids up the chimneys were long afore my time. I'm

46

not a hundred, you know. Anyways, nobody knows what the past's like 'cept them what's lived through it."

I felt the logic of that. Was quite prepared to admit its unassailability—if for no other reason than that my primary concern for myself was not the past but the future. Instinct told me, however, that Mr. Trebilcock was not interested in a discussion with me of the world's post-war future — let alone that of mine, or even his own.

"What was it like when you were my age, Mr. Trebilcock?"

I sat back. Experience plus native cunning had taught me the pacifying nature of certain kinds of questions — when dealing with obdurate uncles and acrimonious aunts.

Old Trebilcock skilfully rolled his bedraggled butt from one corner of his mouth to the other.

"I suppose you'd have called me dreamy as a youngster," he began. "Let's see. I was about your age when? '96 or thereabouts? Anyways, during what they called the naughty nineties . . . ."

He began to drone on and on about the Boer War, the first motor buses. I soon lost interest. Christ! Old men can gab, can't they?

I had already noticed how his heavily veined hands trembled when he took pencil to the galleys in front of him. Now I noticed the effects of shaking fingers upon his face. From a distance I suppose he looked clean-shaven, but an examination from just across that table showed whole furrows of whiskers that had escaped his shaving. Like the last lines of wheat waiting to be mown when a horse-drawn binder has been going around and around a harvest field all day.

But if the bits of missed beard looked unpleasant — that was nothing compared with the dewdrop of snot perched under his nose. I stared at that now. Fascinated at its fight with gravity each time he sniffed it back to the shelter of his nostrils. Crazy, horrible thoughts leaped in me. I wondered how salty it tasted. That idea made me want to retch, of course. I got up.

"Just going to the lav, Mr. Trebilcock," I muttered across the monologue of his unfinished lament for times past. And fled him and the stuffy room for fairer sights.

Downstairs, before I reached the toilet, I found one. A fairer sight I mean. She was a tall girl — taller than me — with hair like Rita Hayworth's in the movies. Down to the shoulders that is. Only black, and full of waves. Very Cornish she looked, with her quick brown eyes and pale, nacreous skin. Spanish-looking, an English person would have said.

" Mornin' then. You'm Davey Bryant I suppose. The new junior reporter?"

I liked that — especially as old Trebilcock had only referred to me as the copy-boy. To her pretty looks I straightway attached a pleasant temperament.

" Yes, I am," I said. " Working up there." I jerked my head towards the broad, uncarpeted flight of stairs behind me. " With Mr. Trebilcock and Mr. Tremayne at the moment."

" Mr. Tremayne's me uncle." She lowered her eyes. Acting shy, I thought.

" You work here at the paper, too, then Miss Tremayne?"

That sounded more formal than I'd intended. But at that time, when talking to girls, my words tended to come out in rushes — with little control from me.

" Yes, I do. And I'm not." She gave a bright little laugh. " I'm in the advertising department, but I'm not Miss Tremayne. He's mother's brother, you see. I'm Audrey Pengelly. We'm from down to Boscarne."

" Oh, yes," I said. " I knew there was Pengellys to Boscarne." (I didn't, but what the hell?).

" Anyway, you must call me Audrey, and I shall call 'ee Davey. We'm all friendly 'roun here. None of that there stuffy nonsense, you."

" I'm glad of that," I said. " 'Tis a bit different up there, you. Though I reckon you know that right enough without I tellin' of 'ee."

As I spoke, broadening my Cornish accent to suit hers, I searched her features. A neat little nose : no dewdrop. Such smooth skin, such a nice smell of lavender-scented powder coming from it : no stubble missed by a razor. I sighed. How I loved the youthfulness which made us peers. And at the same time . . . how I hated age and its strangeness, its ugliness and all the boring things about it . . .

" My! That were some sigh! Feelin' sad then?"

I started. I hadn't realised . . . was surprised she'd noticed.

" No. Not a bit. 'T'other way round, you ! I was getting a bit fed up, up there." I thought quickly over what I'd said. " Not with your uncle, mind. He idn' there now. But ol' Mr. Trebilcock — well 'ee idn' exactly a ray of sunshine, is 'n, you?"

" Him?" Her voice flooded. " Miserable ol' thing 'ee is ! You don't have to tell us ! Idn' one of us girls in Classified that can abide 'un. Nasty, grumpy, messy ole man he is ! An' one of these days, when he do grumble at us, I shall tell of 'un to his face, don' 'ee fret!"

" I lef' un upstairs, natterin' on' bout how much better 'twas in his time than in our'n."

" Tell I news, not history, you ! If tidn' that then 'ees on to 'ow much better Lanson is to Bodmin."

" I had that 'fore he got on to the times when 'ee was young."

" Why don't 'ee get back up there to Lanson, then, eh ? That's what us in Classified 'ud like to know. 'Tis all very well moanin' and frettin' 'bout Bodmin — but he bain't got to stay 'ere, if 'ee don' want to. Tis a free country, idn' it ?"

" I reckon." I loved her indignation. I'd like to see her having a real go at him, I thought, I really would, you.

" Want to meet the other girls, then?"

The relief of her after the old men gave me a peculiar courage. I let our eyes meet.

" Well, tidn' exactly necessary," I said slowly. " I know already there idn' nicer in there than out 'ere."

With grey, pleated skirt below the charcoal grey sweater, she parodied a curtsey. " Well, thank 'ee for the compliment. Only it tripped off your lips so smooth, I bet I bain't the first to hear it, you."

If she had been too pert I would have run scared.

49

But her voice was gentle, encouraging.

" No, I never. I bain't said that to a maid afore. Nor nothin' like it, come to that."

" Really."

Then a longish pause before she spoke again.

" Here, I've got to go! I'll get the sack, talking to you out here."

" What — what about lunchtime?" I said. " What do you do then?"

" We — I — usually go up to Richards and Dyers. For a pasty, you know . . ."

I mentally exterminated the pasty my mother had carefully packed in greaseproof for me.

" Could we go together then? That's what I was g'in do anyway. And my being new and that — there's a lot you can tell I."

" All right, then," Audrey said. " But I must go now or Miss Nancarrow'll be wondering what on earth's happening to me."

So I skipped upstairs again, now much lighter of heart with an anticipation to feed on. In fact I had quite forgotten about going to the lavatory until back at my seat reading the copy back to Trebilcock — when it was too late to do anything about it.

When the old-fashioned clock on the dismal green wall, with its mottled face and genesis of Camelford inscribed in copperplate across it, showed noontime, I thought of lunch —and cursed myself for not asking Audrey what time she went.

". . . . A St. Kew man, George Trelawney, has been decorated for bravery,' " I read.

" All right, all right — let's rest up a minute. This isn't the Irish Sweep you know," old Trebilcock grumbled.

At least I thought he grumbled as he fumbled shakily with the makings of another cigarette and eyed me at the same time.

" Sorry," I said. " Didn't know I was going too fast."

" It's a matter of getting the right pace," he said. " So that we space it out over the whole bloody day for one thing."

50

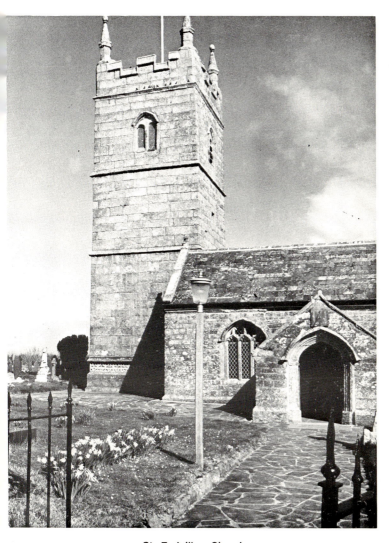

St. Endellion Church

Photo : Ray Bishop

In " Polgy-Wurgy " (Poltrewirgie) Wood

" I see," I said, wondering whether Audrey would think of coming up there to collect me.

"What you doing for lunch, son?" Trebilcock asked abruptly.

I was startled at his reading my thoughts. I also realised that, despite the roughness, it was obviously an invitation.

" I — I don't know. That is — "

" I've decided to let you come with me. Can't usually abide people with me when I'm eating. But you being new and that . . . Well, I'm prepared to make a special thing like . . . ."

"Well, that's very nice, Mr. Trebilcock. Very nice indeed. But . . . It's only — "

" Course, if 'ee don' want to — I bain't a-forcing of 'ee, that's for sure." He spoke fast and forcefully. But somehow the words didn't fit with the look in his eyes. It was those watery things I answered — couldn't help it.

" I'd love to. I just didn't want to push myself on you, that's all."

My vision of laughing Audrey jumbled confusedly there in the fore of my head. With sinking heart I imagined what she'd say. Bound to be upset, cross, after all. Hadn't I just promised her a matter of mere minutes ago?

" You ready then? Better get there 'fore the place fills up. It's like Bedlam when all they stupid shopgirls get in there. They'll push in front of the queue, too, if 'ee don't watch 'em like hawks. No respect for age, neither. Shove right past 'ee — bravun bunch of hussies . . . "

What shall I tell her? That he'd asked me earlier and I'd forgotten? She was hardly likely to believe that! What then? That in a weak moment I'd given in to an old man's begging? After what she'd had to say about his nastiness — and my agreeing?. . . . .

I racked my brain . . . indeed, was still racking it as I walked downstairs behind his carefully descending figure — my eyes held gloomily on that old-fashioned, large-brimmed hat he'd meticulously placed over those dank and dandruffy locks of his.

At least she wasn't in the hallway when we got to the

bottom of the stairwell. But the counter behind which I presumed she worked, faced the long, plate-glass window, and I knew she'd see me as Trebilcock and I walked past up the slope of Honey Street.

Better do something now as we were leaving than try and explain later. I waited till he was actually pushing through the front door of the building before muttering ' Excuse me ' and slipping through the door to the right which led into the front office.

She was examining one of the huge ledgers but looked up and smiled those lovely white teeth as I entered. But the pretty mouth turned down at the edges fast enough as I spoke to her.

" Sorry," I rushed. " There's been a change of plan. My — my granddad just phoned. Wants to have lunch with me as my gran's taken a turn for the worse."

Panicking, as vexation and disbelief frosted her features, I decided to lay it on thicker. " They don't give her very long now, Granddad told me. He's pretty upset — you can imagine."

That final spurt of inventiveness got less attention than it deserved, as at that moment there came a heavy knocking on the plate glass window. I turned quickly. It was old Trebilcock, face furious, banging and beckoning to me at the same time.

" Grandfather's waitin' for 'ee," said Audrey, an unpleasant edge to her voice. " Don' keep of 'un awaiting on account o' me."

I made one more desperate effort. " Old Trebilcock's a friend of Grandpa's. He was going out so I said I'd explain about Grandma on the way to the restaurant."

More window banging. " Can we go tomorrow, then?" I asked. " Sorry 'bout today — really I am."

I don't think I could have stood any more of that racket from the old man out there on the pavement. I was already backing towards the door — hoping the look on my face was beseeching. For whatever reason, it worked. Or something worked, for she suddenly relented : smiled.

" All right," she said. " Tomorrow, an' let's not have a lot of all they fibs then, shall us?"

Nodding, smiling, doing anything that came into my head, I pushed through the doorway and out of her sight. There were no words to offer her last remark anyway.

" See you've already started flirting with that silly bunch in there," was Trebilcock's sour comment as I joined him.

" Her grandfather had a stroke this morning. I thought I should say something," I told him solemnly. And then, just in case that didn't make him feel small enough. " He and my grandma were childhood sweethearts. They've known one another over sixty years."

He didn't speak as we made our way slowly to the restaurant which turned out to be already as crowded as he had gloomed. After muttering his way through the menu and snarling his order to the red-haired waitress (to the accompaniment of a bright-eyed, smiling request from me for a pasty), he conceded once more to my presence.

" You heard what I said out there? Better mind they chits o' girls in the office. One or other'll see you get 'em in the family way — quicker than you can wink!"

I toyed with my knife and fork. If that was going to be his line of talk during the meal, the quicker it was over and we were back reading that boring stuff in the office, the better.

" And if that one said her grandfather was ill, then she were lying! Why old Tremayne would've talked of nothing else this morning. It's his father-in-law, and he hates the ground he walks on."

" Maybe it was Audrey's other grandfather," I ventured.

" Hasn't got one. Died years ago . . . used to have the shoe shop over the road there."

I gave up then. This wasn't my day. I was beginning to doubt whether it was my job either. Life was simpler at home on the farm. You didn't have to lie so much — and there was less danger of being found out.

With my developing silence he seemed to grow gentler.

" Know what happened when I was your age?"

" No, Mr. Trebilcock."

" I got a maid into trouble. Ruined my life in a way. I would've gone to college, you see, if I hadn' had to marry at seventeen. From then on it was work — work with a bunch of me inferiors, what's more."

By now I was bolt upright. He had my attention now, all right. To think of that dried-skin, scarecrow of a man, seducing some girl! It was incredible. I think I must've shaken my head in instinctive disbelief. At any rate, he pushed the pepper and salt shaker close together at the middle of the table and said : " It happened all right. She nagged me for twenty years. Till the 'flu got her in nineteen — or was it 1920?"

" And the child? Your son?"

" Daughter," he corrected. " Her parents brought it up."

" Do you — do you see her much? Now that is?"

I knew that his watery eyes were nothing to do with tears, but as I looked at him I thought that even their pale colour faded.

" Nope."

" I see," I said, feeling stupid.

" I hope you do. That's why I told you. So you wouldn't make the same damn fool mistake."

" I don't think that's likely, Mr. Trebilcock," I countered, the tone flooding back in my voice. " I haven't got too much time for girls, not right now, I haven't. I'm joining the Navy just as soon as I'm old enough to volunteer. Then when the war's over, I'm going to University. There'll be special grants for Servicemen, my dad says. Just so long as the war lasts long enough. That's my only worry."

" These girls — they no sooner look at you than they're scheming. Two of these world wars have killed off so many of the men, the women are desperate. Why d'you think skirts have got shorter, eh? And all that muck on their faces?"

There was enough muck on his face, dried spittle at the turned-down edges of his mouth : obscene hair growing out of the redness of nostrils, a scaley skin . . . But he seemed too down in the dumps for me to argue with him.

" Things are easier now," I said neutrally. I meant — well, I wasn't sure what I meant . . . Maybe that boys and girls understood one another better than either could take the likes of him. Anyway, he chose to believe I was talking about something different.

"Those contraceptives? Those Frenchies? Don't kid yourself they're any good!"

I looked at the tablecloth — focussing particularlly on a large tea stain towards the edge. It looked like the breast of a woman, even to the nipple on the end.

"We had those condoms then. I'm not that old, my lad. But I tell you, nothing's safe. You can't rely on anything or anyone for that matter."

That last bit was more to my liking. "Well, don' 'ee fret, Mr. Trebilcock. I don' rely on anyone for anything. God helps those who help themselves and all that, eh?"

"Well, don't get fooled, that's what I'm telling 'ee. Look what a bloody mess I've made of my life — and learn from it."

"I will, Mr. Trebilcock, I will." (Christ knows I don't want to end up like you! I can't think of anything worse).

When the pasties arrived he was silent for a while. I watched tapering fingers picking out bits of gristle and piling them in an unseemly heap on the side of his plate. I felt sick.

I was beginning to day-dream — mainly about Audrey and our lunch the next day.

"Old Tremayne's got a bad ticker, you know. Had a couple of heart attacks, already he has. I'll see of 'un out. He won't make old bones, you."

I fled from an image of Audrey to a mouth mumbling with pasty and lumps of over-cooked stewing beef. The closest thing to a glint he could manage was there in those rheumy eyes.

"What the drink doesn't destroy, all that stupid excitement over his horse betting will. One or t'other'll finish of 'un off, you mark my words."

What was he crowing about, for God's sake? That one old man was leaving the world in front of another? Your turn to curtsey, my turn to bow?

He must have read the incomprehension that flitted across my face. Or mis-read it rather.

55

"Bored, eh? Don't make no difference to a youngster like you, which of us goes first — then why should it?"

There was no answer to that, and I didn't try one.

"So you intend going to some university when this is all over. Well, I can't offer much advice there. I told you . . . I had to give up any idea like that."

(Mr. Trebilcock, I don't need your advice . . . Don't want it . . . To be perfectly frank, Mr. Trebilcock, not only you but your whole world's over . . . Something new's peeping over the horizon . . . After a few months of what looks like a stupid, boring job with you on the Cornish Guardian, I shall be jolly Jack in the King's Navy . . . Girls falling all over me . . . Then, if the war'll only last out, a commisssion . . . My nice wavy hair under a sporty sub-lieutenant's cap . . .A little ship . . . A corvette perhaps? I shall look better than my cousin Jan 'cause his head's too small for a naval officer's uniform . . . Then, when we've sunk the last Jerry sub, shown those Japs where they get off, some beautiful Oxford college . . . lolling about in punts . . . Flopped out on lawns . . . and girls . . . girls . . . girls . . . A brilliant degree . . . English, of course — what else for a great novelist? And then . . . and then . . . But my unspoken thoughts gave out just there).

The waitress brought us our tea in thick, chipped cups and I had a vanilla ice which I sprinkled with sugar as it wasn't sweet enough. He was talking to the red-haired girl now, complaining about the tea spilt in his saucer. She and I exchanged a glance. Just a quick one. But enough to share a thought . . . Old men! . . . I made an effort.

"No sweet, Mr. Trebilcock?"

He'd already lit one of those filthy hand-made cigarettes of his. "That wartime junk? It's all — what the Germans call it? Ersatz. Why, I doubt whether you've ever tasted a real saffron bun. Just yellow colouring, that's all it is nowadays. Why, I can remember food the likes of which you've never thought of. When I was a youngster — oh, younger than you — I'd eat more at one sitting than you war kids get in a week."

I took out one of the two posh Turkish cigarettes that I'd stuck in one side of the silver cigarette case that mother gave me when Uncle Thomas had gone down on H.M.S. Glorious, and which he'd obviously never needed again. I gave my phoney smile. "Surprised you're not fatter than you are, then, Mr. Trebilcock. I mean, with all that rich food as a boy . . ."

He took me dead on. Seriously that is.

"Well, I was taller than you, my lad, at fifteen. And half a stone heavier I should reckon."

He was now a shrunken scarecrow — bantam weight. Is that what age did?

"Take my birthdays."

(No, you take 'em, Mr. Trebilcock. I never want that many if that's how you have to end up).

But what I actually said was : "How were they then, were they fun?"

He didn't need any prompting, though. He was away down memory lane.

". . . It was August month . . . The seventeenth to be exact. There'd be trestle tables up in the mowey. At least three of 'em. Beautiful damask cloths on 'em too. Not filthy things like this. Real Irish linen. Never see such things anymore . . . Mother'd go all out. A proper old Cornish spread. Pasties of course — turnip and potato. Real beef, mind . . . Not this horseflesh muck . . . Oh, all the usual things. Apple pasties stuffed with cream in both halves. Pies, dozens on 'em . . . Damson, gooseberry, and my favourite, blackberry and apple. Did I mention the jam splits and cream?"

"No, I don't think you did, Mr. Trebilcock."

"There were platefuls of 'em. Mind you, half of Tregadilloc was there. That was the village outside Launceston, where Dad farmed. I reckon, what with the family and relatives, as well as our friends, there were over a score sitting down to my birthday party out there under the elms. Shouldn' be surprised if every one on 'em's gone now, too."

It's funny, but I could imagine him easier a little boy than as a young man. I stared at him, trying to see that time-dried face fresh again in a dead world, under a long-gone sun.

He either sighed or wheezed (it didn't really matter). "They were good days, they were. Nope, I don't envy you, son. Not when I remember times like that, I don't."

Good. The feeling was mutual . . .

Soon after that we took our respective bills and queued up in the lengthy line to get out of the place. In a matter of minutes we were back at that enormous table — me reading, he at his soundless echo of the dreary copy.

" 'Preachers on the North Cornwall Methodist circuit next Sunday will be . . .' "

" 'Pleading not guilty to three offences of criminal assault against a minor, Richard Pocock, 35, unemployed labourer, through solicitor W. M. Menhenniot, argued that a fifteen-year-old schoolgirl had told him she was a member of the Women's Land Army, and consented freely to all three acts . . .' "

The film of recollection runs smooth as cellophane through my mind : The endless recitation of weddings, funerals, whist drives, sexual offences, council meetings, accidents . . . The Cornish Duchy chugging through the sour years of war.

The only break in the diurnal chant, the caustic comments from the emaciated Mr. Trebilcock at the world's stupidity. And the drunken tee-hees of Mr. Tremayne, who by the afternoon thought existence the wildest joke.

The only break? Not quite. After that first black Monday, between the treadmill eight-hour day, five-and-a-half-day-a-week job on the Cornish Guardian, were those islands of delight that spelled Audrey.

Our first lunch . . . All questions and laughing flirtation: the joys of discovering agreed ideas, the fleeting solemnity of combined disapproval of this and that.

The shared train ride to Nanstallon Halt, where she got off each day. The happy findings of a compartment we need share with no one. The breathless pulling down of the shade as we chugged through the luscious foliage of the Camel Valley, blind to the beauty of sunlight on rippling water as we found the beauty of each other and exchanged our first kisses.

Or the Saturday morning two weeks? three weeks?

later, when instead of the Nanstallon faewell, she stayed on the noon train and we both got off at relatively unknown Grogley, and made our way hurriedly past the scattering of granite cottages towards the beckoning meadows at the river's edge.

There were willows there, I remember. Willows and wild irises to shield us from human sight. We lay on the crushed green blades, the yellow blooms so tall above us they appeared black against the fragmented blue of the sky beyond the weeping willow branches.

It was there in the murmur of panted endearments that I finally slipped the shoulder straps of her petticoat down, and her crossed arms formed a " W " of modesty as I sought those pathetically protected breasts. Made coarse, made mad by the taste and tang of her, I searched and researched her body with oafen feverishness. Until in the trembling reluctance of her maidenhead, still whispering ' No ' as her flat white stomach arched in a passion of ' Yes,' I slid through the moist invitation to the depths of her.

In the stillness and quiet that followed, the mother in her made a baby of me. No longer the throbbing male, that scorned her blood and hurt, to crush her with my buttock-tightened weight, I lay instead, my head in the inky fissures of her breasts, as if in womby retreat from what I'd done, as her voice grew stronger in its soothing croon. And nimble woman-fingers stroked my hair.

Oh, there was magic in that moment, sealed in the softness of an April afternoon, when boy and girl entwined in appetite, to make momentary man and fleeting wife of their squirming lusty forms. But after magic there was sadness — sadness and fear as babies clutched each other tight : dimly aware a shore had now been left behind and only repetition called . . .

The sunlight of those months (incredible to me now that they were only months, not years) was slender Audrey. The darkness of the time was summed up in a face whose ever deeper lines were an amalgam of irritation and agony :

" . . . Do you have to fidget like that, Davey Bryant : it's getting on my nerves . . . "

" That's me you're kicking, son, not the leg of the

table . . ."

"That's what they call manners today, is it? In my time things were different, I don' mind tellin' 'ee."

"You'd think no one had ever lived before you, my boy, to hear on 'ee talk sometimes . . ."

"I'm all right, I tell you — don't pester me so . . ."

"It's just a bit of indigestion. Be gone in a minute . . .

"Course I understand what you'm gettin' at. I may look a doddering old fool wi' one foot in the grave — but I've lived, my lad, I've lived. Seen the best o' times and the worst . . ."

Then the goodbye day came. It was Friday. I had to report at the Training Base, H.M.S. King Arthur on Monday morning. My rail pass was made out for Sunday.

Mr. Tremayne did not come in. I never did get the chance to say goodbye to him. With old Trebilcock it was different. Different from how I thought it would be, I mean.

It was all gruffness, of course. That was just as I'd expected it.

"You no sooner get one trained than they're off. And the same damn business has to start all over again."

But there was more.

"Well, don't be as argumentative with they Navy people as you've been here, or you'll soon find yourself in trouble. Take care of number one, lad — no one'll do it for 'ee. Can't say I won't miss on 'ee. You'm not a bad worker when you put your mind to it. Make a good newspaperman one day, if 'ee wants to . . ."

"Here, it's just a little thing. You don't take snuff, of course. But you can use it for saccherin or something. It's real silver . . . belonged to me grandfather . . .

"Now don't keep thanking me. I'm tired of the thing, anyway."

With Audrey all the intended words died between us. On the train to Nanstallon Halt for the last time it was mere litany.

"I love you, Davey."

"I love you, too."

"I'll write, of course."

"So will I."

" Every day, Davey, I'll be thinking of 'ee."

" I'll be thinking of you all the time. It won't be too long, Audrey."

" No, it won't be too long."

" We're here already!"

" Gosh, that was fast."

" Bye, Davey."

" Abbysinia."

" Abbysinia to you, too — darling . . ."

She stood there waving, her white raincoat collar turned up against the penetrating Cornish mist as we chugged round the curve and out of sight.

I never did see you again, Audrey. Others came into your life. Others came into mine . . .

No one saw you, Mr. Trebilcock, for very much longer. They took your body northwards to your native Launceston — never to rail at the world again or to roll a cigarette.

Dear, dead Mr. Trebilcock, who can never die for me — I'm catching you up. I'd like to talk to you now. Now, Mr. Trebilcock. Now . . .

Shipwreck

The May month I went home to Cornwall to bury him spelt silence in Pol'garrow farm, but outside the sadness was all noisy moan : wind creaking elms about the yard, gulls screeching in frustration as they were blown seaward against their wing's wishes, and endless heavy tears from the grey clouds that processed steadily overhead as they made their way inland from a sullen Atlantic.

Out of the foaming surf, far, far below the yawn of Tregardock cliffs, black teeth rose and seized a freighter — blown from its course down the Cornish coast, en route to a gentler English Channel and finally Antwerp harbour. I walked the cowslip-carpeted cliffs the very next day, saw the oil-seeping wreck and watched disconsolate seabirds at nest on the precarious ledges of the cliff-face as walnut-hued fishermen from Port Isaac and Padstow rode the heaving swell in search for survivors.

But sorrow makes selfishness : I looked down on the deserted deck, thought briefly in half-prayer of the drowned men and then of my own dead just freshly sunk below the sloping surface of St. Kew churchyard. With him gone, so was my last connection with this primitive land beyond the River Tamar. I looked into the driving rain, over the grey-green convolutions towards my home. Home? Picking up a sliver of slate I flung it at Canada. Yes, home, in a new and heavier sense as it had never been before.

Behind me, under my feet, in those grey clouds and moaning wind, was the stuff of a home that me and mine had known for centuries. Now no longer.

So I lapsed from my physical sight and saw instead a procession down a lane behind a coffin. And realised as I walked in isolation behind those grim-lipped farmers, that I walked as a family of one . . .

That evening, after numbly munching a cold pasty baked by Mrs. Trebilcock — a pasty that in Vancouver I would have raved over, but which in that damp and silent house I scarcely tasted — I made my way along the sodden path by the hedge, across the wet and slippery stile and down the hill to the Cornish Arms.

" Evenin' Jack."

" Evenin' Mr. Davey."

" Half a Worthington ' E,' Jack. Hullo, Ben. What you having?"

" Pint of mild if 'ee don't mind. Thank you Davey."

I turned and looked about me as I fumbled for change.

It was a neat little pub. Neat and trim. Overhead on the ceiling beams still hung the great hooks which would never see hams suspended again. The hooks on the beams behind the bar held the pint mugs of the regulars. Pewter most of them, some of them glass though. I knew there was one hanging there that would now require a new owner . . .

" Thanks Jack. Cheers then, Ben."

" Cheers you." We ritualised our drinks and bent our necks towards suds. When I looked up my head turned (as everyone else's did) towards the door as someone new entered the tiny room. It was a young man with a head crowned with black curly hair. I knew his face—or thought I did. When the grunts of greetings were done, and he stood next to me with his enormous pint in an earthy hand, I spoke to him.

" I think I know you, but I've forgotten your name."

He looked quizzically, dark Cornish eyes summing up speedily. " No, I don' think. No. I bain't never see'd 'ee before, I'm bravun sure."

" Aren't you, aren't you Wesley Pendorrick?"

A hefty swig of beer and mouth wiping with the back of the hand. I noticed scratches, fragments of dirt at the moon of his nails.

" Father is. I be Daryl."

" I see," I said, drinking at my own glass. I saw only too well. Not for the first time since coming home had I confused two generations by the close similarity of their family features. I found the thought depressing. This reminder of age, that a whole new series of Pendorrick faces, or Jago red hair, or Tremain good looks, had risen to usurp the teen-age freshness of those who had stood there at that very bar and downed their first beer with me.

The face of Daryl Pendorrick spelled future; inevitably, mine must record a journey long embarked on. I thought of who I was, what I had done and finished my glass very quickly.

"Same again Jack. And one for Daryl here." I turned to Daryl. "I remember —"

"Remember what then?" He slid his empty mug casually across the bar to Jack.

But I didn't answer. There was no point in remembering before those who scarcely owned to memories yet. Besides, the sudden vision of Wesley Pendorrick lying with me in the long grass of Boscarrock meadows and the sudden reaching out of hands towards each other in pubescent exploration, was hardly an anecdote to pass on to his son. I blushed as I recalled, in lightning succession, the sequels to that first nervous experiment.

"You'm well away then. Penny for 'em."

I started violently. "I'm — I'm sorry. Just a bag of nothing . . . Childish nonsense. It's always happening to me when I come home."

"Mr. Davey come back for the funeral," Jack the landlord put in—startling me in the realisation he was obviously following our conversation. "You remember ol' Mr. Bryant, Daryl. Always come in here lunch time for half a pint?"

"Course I remember 'un! Now I know who you be then. From over to Pol'garrow b'aint 'ee? You'm a Bryant then?"

I was about to say 'the last of them,' but thought it too melodramatic. "That's right, Daryl."

"I've 'eard all about 'ee."

That raced my pulse, but I needn't have worried.

"Live to other parts, don' 'ee?"

"Vancouver. Canada — you know."

"Like it out there then?"

But I wasn't going through that dreary old routine again. Not right then I wasn't.

"Yes I do. What do you do then? The Pendorricks always used to work at Tregildern, didn't they?"

I noticed the mop of hair dipped slightly — but it wasn't towards the beer mug. When he looked up I thought

64

his eyes were duller.

"Still do. Worked there ever since I left school, you. There's me, father, and me brother Mike." The defensiveness grew louder in his voice. "Tis more open grazin' now, than 'twas. We knocked down pretty many o' they ol' hedges. Spends most of me time on the bloody tractor, you!"

I thought, then, of Tregildern. The square whitewashed farmhouse in the river chuckling dip of the Allan Valley with its land rising steeply, breaking finally free of lush fern lanes and giant elms and merging, in the end with the free-breathing expanse of the moor. Wesley Pendorrick and I had known every field, perhaps every nook that could shelter two squirming bodies . . .

"What do you do, then?"

But all that was just too much to explain. "You like farming then?"

He didn't seem to notice the ignored question.

"Tis a job, you idn' it? Got to do somethin' s'pose."

"You don't seem very keen," I suggested.

Daryl shrugged. "Suits most on 'em round here, I reckon. Me, I do like sheep-shearin', and there bain't enough bloody sheep round here for much o' that."

"Daryl won pretty many competitions for shearin,' 'cluding the Royal Cornwall last year, didn' 'ee Daryl?" As Jack pushed the freshly brimming pint to Daryl I edged my way slightly towards the door lintel, away from the bar. To my satisfaction, Daryl turned in my direction. Now both our backs were to Jack and the possibility of a three-way conversation happily faded.

I sipped and waited for young Daryl to go on.

"Course I shouldn' be here at all, you. Not if it had been up to me, that is."

"Oh?"

"No, Australia, matey. That's where I'd 've gone. If that bitch hadn't put her bloody oar in, you."

"Which bitch is that?" I asked gently.

"Her, o' course. Me bleddy mother-in-law."

The sudden allusion to a mother-in-law with all its stock music hall associations, tempted me to smile.

65

Ignoring my expression, he went on. " That was the beginnin,' you. Her bleddy mother."

I read his face as he talked.

" She've always put her oar in, you. Never was no chance for me and Shirley to work things out. Like that time down to the Royal Cornwall. Th'ole bitch knew'd I was down for the sheep-shearing an' how much I wanted Shirley to be there. Yet there she was the night afore, roun' our place, saying as how Shirl shouldn't go to the Royal Cornwall Show when she was feeling so poorly an' that I should 'ave better things to do an that. Tis always been that way. Hundreds, no bleddy thousands of times, she've interfered . . . "

He even had a gap in his front teeth like his father— and the eyebrows, lithe and quizzical, they were lanes of memory for me in themselves . . .

"Course I can't blame the mother for this last business. I bain't saying that. Blame meself in a way, I s'pose."

I looked at him and remembered standing on top of the disappearing cornmow at fifteen as his father and I fed the threshing machine, our stripped-to-the-waist-bodies, burnished by the sun's glow.

" You do?" I said. " You blame yourself?"

" Maybe I were a bleddy fool not to notice what was going on behind me back between they two bastards. But you don't think that way, do 'ee? I mean not about your wife and your best friend? Course I been told since they been doing things under me nose. Right up to Trevelyan's garage." But as he trotted out the names of persons and places in his domestic drama of a faithless wife and cuck- olding friend, it was, oddly enough, a sense of envy that stirred in me. As the clichéd attitudes of the deceived husband poured from his lips . . . " I'll hit that bugger right on the nose when I do get at 'un . . . Not even his mother'll recognise of 'un when I'm finished . . . I'll teach they two bastards they bain't going to make a fool on me . . . "

And as I heard the litany of beloved names peppering his complaint . . . " They was seen down to Lanhydrock together, Jim Jago seen the bugger's van up to Endellion, and I got mates who've seen of 'em drinking an' giggling

The Cornish Arms, Pendogget

Photo : Ray Bishop

The Bridge at St. K...

up Altarnun pub, and later the same bleddy night all the way down to Egloskerry."

He gave the names as pinpoints to the barbs of his anger, but to me they were simply poems of past association. I spoke to him without opening my mouth, without disturbing the expression of feigned sympathy and attention to his narrative of hurt and humiliation.

' Oh, Daryl, what endless tracts of time and experience separate us. Your pain is my almost-pleasure . . . To be so rich in relationship . . . To have a wife who can be unfaithful, to have friends capable of such beautifully ordinary gestures of disloyalty . . . And all this grief, these ancient blessures of the old monogamistic world, in a cradle of places and people known uninterruptedly for the length of one's life . . .? '

"So I told the maid last night, I did, down to her mother's where her've holed up, tis gin be a divorce my girl — nothing bleddy less than a divorce, I says to her."

"A divorce. You'll start all over again ? Is that it ?" I might have been a secretary, idly repeating the last phrase of a dictated letter.

"No tidn' . . . No it bleddy well idn', Maister."

' But he's dead, Daryl, the final thread whitened and frail in its accumulation of years, withered and snapped in the reaping wind. By an act you are made free, by another act I am made alone. You chose yours : mine was the fruit of that awful inexorability which smells first of disinfectant and finally of nameless, terrible sweetness.'

"I loved her, you see. I reckon I could've known what was happening but didn' want to. She was all I've ever really had, see."

His tone stilled the words in my head, for the first time in a long while I looked him full in the face. In the beershining eyes there was now something else : a softness that talked of tears on an approaching horizon.

"Love?" I said. The word rose reluctant as lead in me. I felt made tired, even by the mouthing of it. Remotely I felt the warmth of the drained beer tankard in my hand and noticed his was empty too. Behind Daryl was a door. Behind that door was a winding country lane . . .

beyond the lane the land shrugged into heathery cliffs and on from there the open sea. In the comet of my mind I sped over that water to where fresh land spelt fresh complexity; pains, problems life and death. I arrived in the white stiff-fingered buildings of Vancouver's West End, and an empty apartment silent with books and sleeping gramophone records. In the explosion of that single second in its twelve thousand mile ricochet, I though of lovelessness. "Here," I said. taking his mug from unresistant fingers, "let's fill these up."

Miffed by his exclusion, Jack filled them and took my money in silence. It suited me. When I turned and crossed once more to Daryl, he was standing there, his farm-roughed hand still outstretched from where I'd taken his tankard. He was looking through me as a few moments before I had looked through the heavy oak door and across the world to the west. He downed a third of the beer in one draught. Then he spoke as if there had been no interruption.

" I didn' love her at first, you. Not at a weddin' time an that. We'd even had the bebby an' her was toddling around afore I knew'd." A half smile softened his face. " I got budgies, see. Good, 'uns — cost ten poun' a pair. It were the first year I was a breedin' of 'em. All they hens was nesting. All on 'em my prize blues. 'Twere one lunchtime. I went in the aviary to feed 'em and clean 'em up a bit. Always do it when I go home then as 'tis too early at half past six when I leaves in the morning for work. I stepped through that door. The hens was flying about, there, all three of 'em. The eggs was due to hatch that same day. Me cockbird too was screeching more than he usually do when I go in. Different noise, you. The buggers was upset, I could tell that right away. Well, I went to the boxes one by one. What 'ee think I found? They'd hatched all right — oh maybe there was a coupla eggs infertile out the three nesting boxes. But every bugger was dead you. Nipped about all bloody and messy. Now I know'd they hen budgies 'll eat their young if 'em's upset, but not three of 'em all the same day. Carryin' bloody coincidence too far that. Then I looked down on the ground and see'd 'un. There was the bugger who done it. A mouse you. A blasted little mouse darting around down there in the sand at the bottom of the aviary. I had 'ee in a twinklin'. Caught 'un by his tail. Well, you little bastard, I told 'un, know what I'm gin do? I'm gin knock your bloody brains out, that's what I be gin do. Then she called to I. I hadn' heard her come out the back door or up the garden. 'Daryl, don't,' she said. Still holdin' of 'un, swinging of 'un round by his tail, I looked at her.

" Know what the bastard's done? 'Eve been and killed every baby budgie in they boxes. Now he's gin get the same."

" ' Please, Daryl,' she says, lookin' at I. ' Tidn't you. Not to kill of 'un like that.' "

He looked me in the eye. " An you know what? I knew'd I loved her then. I dropped that bleddy mouse and she opened the door and he skipped out and away. She — she put her arms round me when I went over to her. Proper upset I was about they budgies. I only had half an hour before I had to get back to work. But sitting there at the kitchen table with her, the baby asleep in its crib, I felt different from what I'd ever known. Yes . . . yes, I loved that maid. And there bain't no one gin tell I different."

For the first time since the misery of my mourning had cloaked me, the distress of another nudged my own core of suffering aside.

" Don't talk of divorce yet, Daryl," I said. " Don't talk of anything while the pain's at its height."

" I don't know why I be boring of 'ee with all this anyways. Don't know how I got off on that tack, you. Tidn' like I. You bein' a stranger an' that."

I found the strength to smile. and it wasn't as hard as I'd thought. " That's what strangers are for, Daryl. Life would be pretty rough without 'em."

He looked at me for a moment in silence. " When be 'ee going out there to Canada again, then?"

" I — I haven't quite made up my mind. Soon. A day or two that is."

" Must be bravun nice out there, eh?"

But it was the reality of his pain I wanted to feed on,

not his politeness. " I suppose so. But I'm really more interested in people than places."

The words were no sooner out than I regretted their pomposity, the stuffy sense of my correcting him. But it was too late. Daryl's mouth stiffened, his eyes lost their warmth.

I remembered his father once more. I was home from the art school in Falmouth — what I would now call graduated and spoke of then as having taken my diploma. On the little train chugging along the sandy tracts of the Camel Estuary between Wadebridge and Padstow, disturbing the sentinel herons, we stood together in the otherwise empty compartment staring out of the open window at the rivuletted sandbanks and across at the harsh white dunes of St. Enodoc. It was our first trip together for several months and I suppose I was moved by a spasm of sentiment. In any event, my hand slipped about his shoulder as we traced the meandering shore of the river. It didn't stay there very long, but in finding him compliant, slipped down to his waist. Then he looked at me, his face a precise replica of the one opposite me now nearly twenty years later. " No, Davey," he'd said firmly. " None o' that no more. I'm getting married August month to Betty up Penhayes."

Like a startled bird my hand had rushed from his person to the shelter of my own pocket. " That's all right, Wesley," I'd said, knowing it was all wrong.

" Reckon I'll be shoving off, then," Daryl said, looking with weasel quickness over me and towards the bar behind. " Nice talking to 'ee. I'll tell Father I met on 'ee."

There was a fraction of silence between us as both sought the rounding off words, the clean parting. But it had to be fragmented, unsatisfactory. A heavy breath from him. " So long then."

" Good bye."

" See 'ee again, maybe, before you'm off."

" I expect you'll find me in here. It's just over the road."

" Evenin' then. Night Jack. Night all."

The small chorus. " Night Daryl." And he was slamming his mug on the bar top and out the door.

I took my smaller mug over, too. Misunderstanding my action, Jack immediately began to fill it again. I didn't feel like telling him.

" Nice boy, that Daryl," Jack said presenting me with a brimming half pint I didn't want.

" Very nice," I said. " I knew his father years ago. They look alike."

" Do 'em?" said Jack, pleasing me rather than agreeing. And I remembered that Jack was from St. Tudy, a neighbouring village. He wouldn't have known Wesley when he was Daryl's age.

I drank up my final beer and made my way slowly through the honeysuckled Cornish night to an empty house . . .

Ashes for Easter

In the March vigour of a Cornish spring I stared contentedly past flimsy muslin curtains to the rockery awash in the morning sun. Years before I had built that rockery: had staggered with the granite stones from the car boot to that site below the stone wall.

Helped by my brothers Tom and Joe, I had piled and patted the mound of earth on which the boulders were to finally sit. Then the casting around for special plants and flowers to splash colour between the silvery grey stones. The wild daffodils that swayed there now were from the orchard of Pol'garrow Farm — their small white bulbs easily uprooted from the loose black loam beneath the apple trees. Joe had gone with me for them. They were still in bloom, I remembered. It must have been about the same time of year.

Joe had still been in Dental School. Now fiftyish, fat and raising a second brood of children and quarreling with a third wife, I doubted whether he could lift one of those boulders that had sunk to deceptive size in the earth, through the years.

Then, though, he had been lean, fresh-faced and full of energy: challenging me at every point over the proportions of the rockery, the disposition of the granite stones, the kinds of rockery plants. I shrugged. Joe had changed . . . So had I . . . So had the rockery . . . I stared out at a clump of pink sea-drift which Tom and I had collected from the clifftop near Pentire Head. Change? Well, who hadn't changed in the twenty years or more since the rockery had been built?

Playing in the rooms of that house, pushing our way laughing through the tamarisk hedge, chopping firewood in the linney, mowing lawns, squabbling over toys . . . my brothers had been my best friends. Now we were all three complete strangers. You can't change more than that, I thought. And sighed, my nose to the cold glass of the window, as mother walked in with a cup of coffee.

" Here you are, Davey. There's a biscuit in the saucer.

72

You like the chocolate ones, don't you? It's funny, Tom always went for the gingerbreads. And Joe . . . Joe would stick to my cake — provided the top was burnt enough, that is, and I hadn't used candied peel. Remember that, Davey?"

"And we'd **all** scream if you put in any marzipan! 'Course I remember! As a matter of fact I was just standing here remembering building that rockery out there. We all three did it — a Saturday morning. It was about this time of year because the daffs were out then, too."

"Davey?" There was something about her voice which made me turn fully around, away from the living room window.

"Yes, mother?"

"There's — there's something I had in mind for you to do when you came home."

"You mean you waited for me to come all the way from Vancouver? My goodness! Must be special!" I spoke lightly but I knew she was having difficulty in getting something out — something that was important, maybe even painful. My mother, diminutive, in her mid-seventies, never had hesitations in speaking frankly. Her shyness never frustrated her candour. "It's — it's to do with your daddy."

I knew it was. She'd been a widow for little over a year. Once, when 'phoning from British Columbia, I had heard her sob a little : the first time her voice had caught in my hearing since childhood. My presence there, at that moment, was largely to do with finding out how she was coping with widowhood, with the new loneliness . . . She busied herself rearranging some African figurines that she and my father had brought home on successive visits to my brother in Nairobi.

"It's something I'd rather you not bother the others with — I mean there's no need for you to tell either Tom or Joe." I just waited.

"It's his ashes, Davey. I've got them here."

"You mean — in the house? Here at Tregildern?"

"I brought them back after the funeral — from the crematorium. He wouldn't have wanted them left in London, you know that."

" No. He'd want them in Cornwall all right."

" Over the parish was what he always used to say."

" Where? Where've you —"

" Got them? In the bureau over there. I didn't really know what else to do, you see. I mean I can't get out in the fields any more, Davey. Not with my legs acting up. Then there's no one left round here I'd like to ask — I mean not for something as personal as that. Then — when you wrote to say you were coming . . . "

" Well, of course I will. It's just the thought — "

" Your daddy was the last one to be sentimental about death, you know. When he wasn't saying he'd like his remains scattered, he was telling me to fling them in the dustbin!"

" I tell you what, I'll take them this morning. It's Sunday, and there'll be fewer people about. I want to take the car to get the newspapers anyway."

" Will you then, dear? I'd be very grateful. It's been on my mind a bit — you know . . ."

I got up and kissed her. " Don't be daft — thanking me! I'd love to do it for Daddy, you know that."

When she turned from stooping and handed me the package wrapped in extremely stiff brown paper, I was surprised at its weight. An official-looking label was stuck on one side, and I held the parcel up towards the light from the window in the dim room, and read the inscription : ' Name — Joseph Trebland Bryant . . . Deceased's remains cremated June 21, 1968. The City Crematorium, Isleworth Cemetery,' etc. . . .

" You know what, Davey?"

" No. What?"

" It's Easter Day, isn't it? Couldn't be a nicer time,"

I clutched the package under my arm. " No, it couldn't," I agreed, and made for the door.

Driving the rented Ford Cortina into Wadebridge (for some reason I had decided to get the Sunday newspapers first), the parcel would not stand on its base, but kept falling over in front of the bucket seat next to mine. It bothered me vaguely lying there, the white label with its funereal lettering staring up from the black rubber mat on the car floor.

Just before I reached the man who sold his newspapers on the deserted Sabbath sidewalk, I pulled over to the kerb of Wadebridge's main street. Taking off my jacket, I draped it as casual-looking as possible over the carton of ashes. It looked decidedly suspicious to me, but I couldn't think of anything else I could do.

When I eventually lowered the window and asked for the two newspapers the vendor, thank God, looked right into my face. " Observer and Sunday Times," he repeated; " Brave bit of reading there, boy, for a sunny day. Should be out walking, you, gettin' a bit o' air in your lungs — not stuck over they ol' papers."

I handed him the money and made sympathetic grunts in my throat. That kind of inane remark always confounded me.

" Bit windy, though, without your jacket on," he added suddenly, nodding towards my coat on the floor. " Need that on if you'm walking the cliffs, you. 'Twill be bravun fresh up there on a day like this."

I revved the motor, sweating in nervousness. If he hadn't stuck his fool head halfway into the window I'd have slammed the car into gear and departed in a swirl of dust. But even manslaughter, added to the illicit disposal of mortal remains, was something I could certainly do without.

" Down here for the Easter holidays, then?"

'Garrulous fool,' I thought. " Yes," I said. " Yes, I'm here on holiday."

" Will 'ee want they two papers next Sunday then? Shall I put 'em aside for 'ee?"

" For the next month," I breathed, edging the car slowly forward. " I've got to go now. Got to meet someone," I lied.

He was still standing there on the kerb, I saw through my rear mirror, as I moved towards the railway crossing. I hoped he was thinking of the few shillings he would make over the upcoming Sundays rather than of that mysteriously draped sports coat on the car floor . . .

Twenty minutes later found me parking the car in the

gateway of Pol'garrow Farm. I'd be in no one's way I realised, as I switched off the ignition, for that track led only to that empty farmhouse where my father had first discovered the world — and where he'd subsequently brought his wife and sired the three of us.

I had always thought it was the most beautiful farm in all of Cornwall, but for the past fifteen years that once child-teeming farmhouse had been silent. All the farmers in my family had died off.

Even five years of unhabitation can be fatal to a domicile in that moist and fecund Cornish climate. I wasn't surprised, then, to note a daintier version of a jungle sprawl had been at work. Ivy and periwinkle swarmed over windows, tiny saplings sprouted amid the mossy hillocks of a perpetually damp roof, tongue ferns flourished in clogged gutters — and, imprisoned in unheated rooms behind dank cob walls, I could imagine the Cornish mustiness, smelling like yeast and stale cheese.

With my bulky package clutched under my coat, I tiptoed carefully over the moist ground. Though Pol'garrow stood empty, a neighbouring farmer had use of the land. It was his scarring tractor treads that had churned up the soft grass approach.

If it hadn't been for the sunny brilliance of the morning, the rich mosaic of greens in the freshness of spring growth, then the dilapidated farmhouse with its caved-in roof, which for centuries had housed the yeoman history of my father's family, would have certainly depressed me. But now I experienced a not unpleasant melancholy over the relation of Pol'garrow, at this stage of its dissolution, to the parcel I clutched tightly out of sight and which I was about to open.

Where the granite outcropping created an island in the surrounding mud, I stopped and carefully opened the paper at the neck. As the covering came free to flap in one hand, I found I was clutching in the other what looked like an outsize milk carton. First, though, what to do with the wrapping? It was so stiff it wouldn't bunch easily in the hand.

I finally got it, if not exactly a neat ball, at least crumpled up enough to stuff in my jacket pocket.

When I had fiddled for a few seconds I got the carton lid open — only to find a folded document lying on top of the ashes themselves. This turned out to be a rough duplicate of the paper attached to the outside and proclaimed my father's full name, the place of his incineration and — somewhat superfluously — the fact that he was deceased.

Conscious that the document was dusty with the contents in which it had been partly embedded, I could only fight my distaste and stuff that paper too in my pocket. The pressing business was the emptying of that brimming container, and I looked about me at bushes and trees to see by their swaying which way the wind was blowing. Briskly, it seemed to me, from the ocean in an inland direction.

I took a few steps westwards, towards the Atlantic, opened the lid fully and lifted the package preparatory to letting the wind waft my Dad's dust across his ancestral acres.

I paused. Perhaps a prayer was called for. Some little religious articulation that was in harmony with what I was about to do? My father had always loved Evensong among the church's services — what better, then, than the Nunc Dimmittis which all five of us used to sing together in that ancient oak pew of St. Kew Church. " Lord, now lettest Thou Thy servant depart in peace/according to Thy Word/ For mine eyes have seen/Thy salvation/which Thou hast prepared . . . " I stopped; for one thing I wasn't sure whether I could remember it all. For another, I had an uneasy feeling that what I was singing was redundant. He had already been sent from this world with the benisons of Holy Church. I was surely confusing the ministrations of the priest with that of a sexton. Action was required here — not words. With that I lifted the cardboard container to shoulder height and jerked it forward so that the ashes would spill out. They did. Some of them even got lifted by the wind and a small grey cloud floated towards the grass-sprouting hedge that bordered the farmyard from an adjacent field.

But then I happened to look down towards the ground. What I saw made me wince. Apart from the fact my brown suede shoes had themselves taken on the pallor of death, the churned clay through which I'd just picked my way, now had a narrow grey swath of my father's death-dust clearly delineated across it.

Nervous, upset, I tried again, lifting the carton head-high and jerking its contents out even more fiercely. Again a misty grey patch drifted away from me — but this time the quantity falling immediately to the ground, to make stark dry patterns, was even greater.

To make things worse, I either stepped forward too quickly or the wind veered slightly. At any rate I felt the gritty particles from the package brush against my face, sensed their rubbing against my hair line. I panicked a little. I tried for a second to scatter the ashes on the ground with my toe — to mix them with the mud, that is. It didn't work. Apart from a yet more scruffy toecap, the only result was the conviction in me that if anyone walked in from that lane and looked about where I was standing he would say at once that someone had been there recently scattering human remains about the mud and dung of a farmyard.

Jamming the lid folds closer together, I fled from that hummock of granite back to the car to try somewhere else.

Inside the Ford, after re-combing my hair and wiping my face with a handkerchief, I looked once more at the contents of the container. With a sense of gloom I discovered that scarcely a quarter of my father's remains had been yet disposed of.

Tight-mouthed, I moved the car forward, thinking furiously all the time of an alternative site to finish the task I had promised my mother I'd perform.

The place I finally came up with was a small granite quarry which my family owned and had once worked. It provided, I recalled, a superbly panoramic view of St. Kew church and the village nestled about it.

"You'll never beat that, son," my dad used to say, standing there by Uncle Petherick's quarry and gazing out on Cornwall. "Most beautiful sight in the world, Boy — and I seen the Sphinx and Gallipoli too in the Great War, don't forget. Ancient human roots in an ancient land — that's the secret, Davey. 'Tis a proper old job, you, isn't

it?" Then he'd grin. " Better than that old Canada of yours,
I reckon!"

With a quick glance about me as I got out of the car,
to make sure I was alone up there, I grabbed the carton
and walked hurriedly away from the massive wall of
granite which formed the quarry's face. By climbing
up on the eastern edge of what formed a rough amphi-
theatre I found myself in the brightness of a momentarily
uninterrupted sun.

A large spread of the Cornish peninsula seduced my
eyes until, when I tilted my chin and I searched the horizon
of clay tips over towards St. Austell, their white pyramids
merged with the dazzling whiteness of a sun-shot haze.

Just as I stood there, growing contentedly aware that
I had come to the spot that surely my father himself would
have chosen, there came, caught on the brisk wind playing
about my head (which brimmed my eyes with tears), the
abrupt clash of bells proclaiming Eastertide. Louder and
louder, or so it seemed to me, the sound swept up from
that gorgonzola'd tower which, in a matter of weeks, would
be entirely screened by the foliage of the surrounding elms.

Once more I was constrained to join my voice with
that of the Church now pealing from tower to tower at
eleven o'clock across the valleys and hills of Cornwall.
    " Hail thee, Festival day
    Blest day thou art hallowed forever "
— and with that I opened full the neck of the carton and
flung the final dust of my father to join the earth, the wind
and the sky, which had initially served in his shaping.

With a wonderful, an exhilarating sense of completion,
I saw those grey particles hover, just for a second, in the
hand of the breeze — then vanish into the broader realms
of the parish below.

Some dust went on me, I suppose. But now I no longer
cared. What was I, after all, than a later echo of that
earthen womb down there?

Then, not the wind, but some inner sadness squeezed
my eyes. " Good-bye, Daddy," I said. And then, because
afraid of the daftness of sentimentality from extempore
words, I said the line, the opening line of his favourite

hymn : "The day Thou gavest Lord, is ended." I would have said more except my chest was filled with emotions that allowed no space for air. As the bells pealed and pealed, rooks cawed and other birds sang. Distantly, lambs bleated. I wanted it to go on and on — forever . . . .

Feeling the sun as a faint warmth on my closed lids, I gave the carton a final jerk — like oldtime sowing of wheat being broadcast across a ploughed field. At the same time I found breath to conclude with another handful of churchy words : " Glory be to the Father, and to the Son, and to the Holy Ghost. As it was in the beginning, is now and ever shall be . . . World without end . . . Amen . ."

I opened my eyes. The bells had stopped. A large cloud was trespassing on the blue space the sun occupied. In a moment, I realised, the land would be in shadow. I looked at my hand still stretched out and at the carton held in it. I gave the thing a jerk, it rattled. There were a few bits left in the bottom. For some reason they gave me the creeps in a way the ashes in my hair and on my face had not. Perhaps it was some fragments of bone that didn't incinerate? Anyway, something unpleasant. I wasn't going to peer in to find out.

Now, of course, I had to dispose of the carton itself. That, and the brown paper covering stuffed in my coat pocket — oh yes, and also the label with its formal description of the contents.

Away to my right the land veered sharply, almost precipitately, down towards the lush valley of the ambling Amble river. But there, at the top, the vegetation was thick thorn scrub before opening up onto a bleak outcrop of heather, gorse and bracken — moorland in fact.

As a sturdy thirteen-year-old, a member of the St. Kew Scout Troop, I had tried unsuccessfully to push through that mass of blackthorn, now just beginning to foam with blossom. With all my strength I flung the carton into the impenetrable midst of it. By the time those branches were bare again, the sun, the wind and the rain would have dissolved that cardboard composition.

Satisfied that it had entirely disappeared, I crumpled the brown paper covering once more, and hurled that in the carton's **wake.**

Brushing my hands on my jacket lapels, I turned back towards the car in the shadow of the cliff-face. I felt a paper in one of my pockets. It was the document I'd discovered in the neck of the parcel on first opening it. Carefully I folded it small, stuck it in my wallet.

Then I turned for home and my mother : able now to tell her the thing was accomplished. The cycle wholly completed.

Only months and months later, walking a Vancouver beach with my dog, staring out from Kitsilano at a westering sun across the Pacific, did I bring to light that piece of folded paper from the recesses of my billfold. I rolled it into a tight ball with the palms of my hands. Then I flipped it lightly with forefinger and thumb, out across the water. My bassett hound, Wendy, saw it, and made as if to retrieve it. But the rippling tide put her off. She never has been that keen on water, nor even with retrieving, come to that.

To divert her, I ran quickly along the flat sand of the beach, calling to her. Soon she was baying at my heels and we ran until we were both puffing.

I never did look back to see whether that scrap of paper had finally sunk below the small waves . . .

Cousin Petherick and the Will

PART ONE

" Where be goin'?" my Uncle Wesley asked me, looking up from the supper table, his mouth full of pasty, his beefy farmer's hand clutching a yeast bun he was tackling simultaneously.

" Up field," I lied smoothly, my plans well prepared, such questions anticipated. "' I want to get Aunty some daffodils from Tregildern Meadows."

" Cows isn't let out yet. Work idn' over wi' milkin', you know."

" I'll do it on my way." That was what I intended.

He looked up fully from his plate, lips littered with pastry, his brown eyes hard with disbelief. " That's likely, that is! Well, be back afore dark. Ducks wasn't shut up last night. An' that fox was about. You can shut the fowls up too, when 'ee comes through Wayfield."

I stared at him, trying to keep my face passive. That was in the opposite direction from the path I intended taking — but I had no intention of letting him know that. I think he took the look as a reproach, though.

" I can't do everythin' with your aunt away, you. I got they bloody books to do. She hadn't even entered the egg money or the milk money afore she went into hospital."

Normally I'd have defended her. If an aunt with suspected cancer needed defending! But that would have taken up time — and maybe even another row and my being forbidden to leave the farmhouse at all, except to do his bloody chores.

" Right, Uncle Wesley. Soon be back."

And I was off to see Second Cousin Petherick, the man I think my Uncle Wesley despised most in all the world.

Now a bit about Cousin Petherick . . . Well, to start with, he was the same age as Uncle Wesley, that's to say in his late fifties, while I was sixteen, coming on seventeen. And he was unmarried. Now, as far as my uncle was concerned, the trouble started right there. Throw in the fact he owned the farm where we lived, many of the cottages down in the village, and that he was as ardent a worshipper in our parish

Street Scene, Bodmin

Photo : Ray Bishop

Cliffs at Port Quin, St. Endellion Parish

Photo : Ray Bishop

church of St. Endellion as Uncle Wesley was a supporter of the local methodist chapel, and you have more than enough ingredients to feed Uncle's ready antagonism.

Those were the perpetual constituents of dislike that invariably sparked the hostility that seemed to flare, more often than not, when each month Cousin Petherick arrived at our farmhouse porch to collect the rent.

But behind all that were other things : tensions, dark jibes and jabs locked somewhere in their personal histories, preserved in some aspic of hate from long before my birth. It was this that fascinated me, this that had arisen a few nights earlier when Petherick had come and old scandals involving unknown names had reached my ears as I skulked, safely out of sight, in the back kitchen. This, indeed, which took me now, still abrim with curiosity, to the isolated hamlet of Polquite where Cousin Petherick lived alone in his comfortable cottage.

He was out in his garden, picking masses of white and purple lilac, as I pushed my bike through his gateway.

" Why, hullo Davey. How be 'ee, my 'andsome ? "

Cornishism must be met by Cornishism, I decided.

" Proper," I said. " Been wishy weather though 'av'n 'er ? "

" Good for lilac boy. Come on in and 'elp I put it aroun,' will 'ee."

Cousin Petherick wore a thick grey flannel shirt (he never wore a tie) and faded blue denims that I secretly thought looked ridiculous on his huge, fat bottom.

Picking up another bunch he had placed on the fresh-mown lawn, I followed him into his double-fronted cottage where a blazing elmwood fire flamed in his sitting-room, sending a flickering glow about the chintz chairs and sofa, and shadowing the creamy walls beyond.

" Thought I'd light the fire, you. There's a brave ol' nip in the air, spring or no spring."

The chat was as innocuous as that as we broke off twigs and surplus leaves and I helped him to decide on vases and their disposition about the snug room. Only when we had sat down and Petherick crossed his legs and beamed at me did I start my careful probing.

"You know, when I've finished with school, Cousin Petherick, I think I'll leave Cornwall and go up country. I don't know England at all, you. Where do 'ee think I should go? You spent a lot of time up there in the past, 'aven't you?"

"What about the farm, boy? Thought you was g'in be the farmer in the family."

"That can wait. I should see a bit of life afore I bury meself down 'ere, I reckon. You did, didn' 'ee?"

Petherick uncrossed his legs. "Yes, I s'pose. Back before the war, that is. Well, I'm all for experience, Davey, you do know that."

I aimed for nonchalance. Now was the time to extract the first piece of information to illumine one of Uncle Wesley's dark digs. "Were — weren't you to Bournemouth, or some such place?"

Petherick's eyes narrowed a little. I thought he sat more stiffly in his chair.

"Who told 'ee that, then?" (It came fairly casually but I wasn't deceived).

"Oh, I don't know. I think it was Aunty, or maybe you mentioned it yourself sometime."

"Used to go up there for me holidays. That was years ago, though."

"Why Bournemouth then? We got family there?"

"Nooooo." He gave a funny little smile. "Not exactly. I — I had a friend there. From down here originally, he was. Helped me get a job in a hotel — when jobs was bravun' hard to come by. I weren't no more'n one and twenty. Stayed three years, I did. Then I come home when Mother was first poorly. After that, like I said, I went back jest for holidays."

I looked at my hands — my mind at ninety miles per hour. "What — what happened to your friend, then? I don' think you ever made mention of him before."

Tiny little muscles seemed to be working at the temples of Petherick's fat face: the tip of his tongue ran lizard-like around his lips.

"Bain't nothin' to tell."

"I . . . I was there — out there in the kitchen — when

84

you was talkin' to Uncle the other night."

" Yes ? "

" Well, like I overheard."

" What did 'ee overhear, Davey ? "

I felt trapped. For one thing I hadn't really heard anything specific. Just hints and that. And what my imagination had done with the fragments . . . well, there was just no way I could repeat those things. I think I must have reddened to the roots of my hair. Because Petherick did a strange thing. He got up, came across to me and put his hand on my shoulder. He'd never done that in his life before.

" Tell me what he said, Davey."

Bluff was all I had left.

" Oh you know, about Bournemouth and that. And some name kept coming up. Bill wasn't it ? Bill Jago ? Would that've been your friend ? "

Petherick's hand fell away from me and I sort of felt his size collapsing there in front of me.

" Know what he is ? A vile and vicious man ! A-bringin' up of which he don't know nothing ! — Nor never did !"

That was safer ground for me.

" He's got a spiteful temper, Uncle has — you bain't got to tell I that !"

Petherick crossed the room, away from me, and seemed to be looking at the row of blue volumes of his World Encyclopaedia. " The trouble with your Uncle Wesley is that he do despise me and is jealous of me at the same time. And a man what is jealous of someone he do despise is in some state, you. He'd do anything to get at me. Usually it were through your Aunt who I count me best friend. But what with poor Muriel down there to the hospital, he had but to fling his hatred in me face."

' He . . . he was making it all up then ? 'Tweren't true about . . . about . . .'"

My voice drifted off into the clock-ticking silence of Petherick's parlour. The quiet seemed to amass, like clouds piling up over Roughtor, on the moors, until it was so thick I could hardly believe it would ever be broken again.

My stout cousin kept his back to me as he scanned

the two or three rows of books, around where the Encyclopaedia lived. 'He's getting out a dirty book,' I thought. 'He's going to give me something to read.'

I clenched my hands on the chair arms and wriggled my left foot where it hung suspended from being crossed over the other. But suddenly he turned away from his two bookshelves empty-handed, a frown on his face.

" 'Ow old are 'ee Davey ? "

(As if he didn't know !) " Seventeen come August month. Same age as your niece, Betty, to Boscastle. You always used to call us the twins, remember ?"

That was all just words, of course. Inside me disappointment spread like damp. But I kept looking hard at him, my face not telling him anything I hoped.

" You decided whether you'm Church or Chapel then ? Can't go to both forever, you."

(What a stupid question ! As a matter of fact I'd decided ages ago before that I didn't believe any of it — but that wasn't for public knowledge. Not in Cornwall it wasn't !)

" Church, of course," I said quickly. " Same as you. I'm always in the choir for Evensong, bain't I ? "

" Then — then you should have a talk with Father Henton. That's better than up to Zig-Zag Chapel where they b'aint got an education to spread between 'em."

I uncrossed my legs.

" What you mean ? To talk about you ? 'Bout what Uncle Wesley were saying."

That shook him, just as I intended it to.

" No, no, no. 'Bout life. 'Bout yourself. That's what priests is for, you."

" But we were talking about you."

" There idn' nothing to know about me. That's the trouble. Nothing never happened for me. I had no one to talk to, mind, when I were your age."

" No more have I. That's why I thought . . ."

" You got friends, bain't 'ee ? Down to school ?"

" I'd rather talk to you. They haven't lived, you."

" Tidn' jest living, Davey. 'Tis the learnin' what should go with it that do count."

86

I decided to take just a little risk of revealing myself.

"My friend Wilfrid, down to school. You don't know of 'un. He and I do sometimes talk. Then 'ee's bravun' sharp, you. He's going up Exeter to College for his teacher training when he's finished to Bodmin."

"I bain't talking 'bout book learnin' so much. I got me Encyclopaedia and I reckon I've read half the books the van do bring up from the County Library. But there's things they books don't cover. An' 'ere I am a livin' witness to it."

"What kind of things?" I asked, crafty as ever. (Determination should have been my second name. I wasn't a Bryant for nothing!)

"Oh you know . . . there's religion for one thing. A man can't live wi'out that, Davey. Now there's one thing I've learned."

"All right. What else?"

But I couldn't break into him.

"You'll learn soon enough."

"That's what I'm trying to do? That's why I come up here this evenin', if you want to know."

That got through, I think. At least, he started to move about the room, not looking at anything really. Just sort of walking towards the corners and coming back in the middle again.

"I wish your Aunt Muriel weren't down there to Tehidy. She's a lovely woman, Davey. One day 'ee'll realize that — more'n you can now."

"I'm very fond of Aunty," I said, full of Sunday-school smarm.

"Your Uncle's vicious, and 'ee haven't been all he should to Muriel. But there's reasons. Way back. There's reasons."

"I don't want to talk about Uncle Wesley," I told him, though goodness knows where I got the nerve. "I want to talk about you and your friend. The one up to Bournemouth."

"Bain't nothin' to tell. 'Ow many times 'ave I got to tell 'ee that? I'm here to Polquite and he's upcountry. That's all there is to it."

"Didn't sound that way to me. Not when you and

Uncle Wesley was going at it th' other night."

I didn't know his anger was so near. I'd never seen anything fierce touch Cousin Petherick before. His chins quivered, both his hands stuck out from his barrelled girth and shook in jerky little up and down movements.

"Gossip," he hissed. "You'm just like the rest on 'em! Feedin' on made up lies and viciousness 'bout things you know nothing nor never will. Now why don't 'ee go home and leave I be? Ask your uncle. He'll feed on 'ee wi' what you want to hear, don' 'ee fret!"

I didn't know there were tears in my own eyes until I suddenly couldn't see him properly as he stood there, shaking like an unhappy jelly.

"Twadn' like that," I choked, "Twadn' like that at all. I wanted to learn. That's all. I jest wanted to learn."

I must have started to sob because he came up and shook my shoulders.

"Stop it, Davey. 'Tidn' no good that. Now hush yoursel'. . . ."

"Me and that Wilfrid. We . . ."

"Stop it! I don't want to hear nothin' of it."

"You . . . you and your friend . . . did 'ee? — Was you?"

But whatever had sparked in him had now gone away again.

"Best leave, Davey," he repeated, only almost a whisper now. "I can't 'elp of 'ee. If only 'ee'd realize."

"Why, why?" I persisted through sobs.

His funny little mouth stopped trembling and his wings went down to his sides.

"I got one thing to tell 'ee, Davey. An' when I've told on 'ee I don' never want 'ee to come here alone again, understand?"

I nodded my lie.

He had to find spittle for his mouth to launch his next words.

"I'm fifty-nine come May Day — and you know what I am? He brought his huge head close to mine. I could see little veins like the Camel estuary at low tide, along the bones that held up those podgy cheeks. Hairs on 'em too. Tiny ones. And his breath smelt awful.

" I'm a virgin. I bain't never touched a body — nor none's touched mine. Not . . . not since I stood out there in the galvanize bath and Mother washed me down as a tiny tacker."

His words fell out then, on the heavy breathing.

" I bain't never seen a man or woman as nature made 'em — 'cept for children. An' never touched the privates of no man or woman save me own."

He leant away from me, got balanced on his feet again. " Now leave me be. Like what I said. Leave I please."

Which I did. With no more words : walking quietly out.

PART TWO

Being the last Will and Testament of Petherick Bryant. ' I am writing this in my own hand without Mr. Thody of Trebilcock, Bassett & Thody, seeing as I don't want any lawyers knowing about my affairs while I'm still living. But I have been told that this Will is legal if I get someone else to sign it. Which I have. And I want Mr. Thody to read it here in my living-room at Polquite where I come to all the decisions that I write down here. I'm writing this Will in place of one I've just torn up because Dr. Menhenniot gave me some bad news yesterday. He told me I got Parkinson's Disease and because I've read that up in the Encyclopaedia and know that my hand shaking may stop me being able to write before too long, I want to get this down before that happens.

Everything to be sold-up. I am dividing up what I got in tenths, like the Bible says. One tenth of my estate goes to the heirs of my cousin Elizabeth Barnicott, deceased, and one tenth to my niece Dorothy Oldroyd to Bodmin. One tenth of all monies realized to be divided between my nephew Leslie Trelooe in Falmouth and two-tenths to my second cousin Davey Bryant in Vancouver, Canada.

The remainder, that is five tenths or half my estate is to go to Jimmy Pengelly, eldest son of Harry Pengelly of the Parish of Endellion, who used to work for Father. Jimmy is a fine and outstanding young man who has made a good name for himself as footballer and athlete, as well as playing for the St. Udy Silver Band and bringing pleasure to many. I have watched young Jimmy grow up, and he has been a great consolation to me in my recent years. He don't know nothing of this Will, but I know that as an upright Christian boy he will be a marvellous steward of this world's goods in the eyes of the Lord. I do truly love him and know he has the gift of love himself, which he has truly shared with me. He took loneliness away from me, which is more than I can say for others.

Given by my hand on this 1st day of May, 1960, in my seventy-first year.

(Signed) Petherick Bryant.'

PART THREE

Our coastal sun is rarely fierce in British Columbia, but it can still bemuse. When it pushes away our panoply of cloud, bleaches our log-strewn strands, and blues our sea, it holds us easily in its thrall.

With such a sun on such a beach on Galiano Island, I lay in the summer of '71, dreamily watching the foaming ferry chug through the shadows of Active Pass. Gulls screamed and swooped about her bubbly wake. The sharp trumpet of her echoing horn followed by the steady throb of her engines were the only mechanical sounds to filter through the swish of surf and reaching my ears.

I was thinking of nothing — a great Gulf Island occupation — when I heard a girl's voice calling my name. I didn't have to turn to recognize who it was. Only Tessa sounded like that. The funny little rasp in her throat : part nervousness, part vocal chords. And part, I sometimes suspected, part polished device to go with the elfin image suggested by her small body, and wide, wide eyes, under the cascading black hair.

" I'm here, Tessa. Below the arbutus."

The rustle of leaves meant she was pushing through the red sinews of the arbutus bush. Then my sight travelled up the tanned bare legs, avoided looking underneath the peasant skirt, and met the enormous gray eyes that blinked in the sand-dazzling sunlight.

"What a place! You always find nice nests."

She sunk down next to me.

"Here, this came for you. Ken forwarded it. I guess he thought you were staying at the cottage with me."

She made no effort to hide the reproach in that, but I refused to hear the plaint. Concentrated instead on the pale blue envelope held in her hand.

"Can I have it then?"

"Sure. I wouldn't have dared invade your retreat without a proper excuse."

I knew she was watching me with sweeping glances (hungry looks?) as I eyed the British stamp with excessive care and tried to decipher the smudged postmark. I probably pursed my lips in awareness of her sitting there, legs crossed in pixie pose. At least, my friends tell me that's how my mouth goes when something is irritating me.

"It's from Cornwall," I said.

"I know. You told me that's where Bodmin was. And I worked out the postmark. At least the BOD."

The words 'quizzy bitch' flitted through my head as I tore the letter open — making rather a hash of the envelope as I did so. Then I forgot Tessa and her needs as I read the rounded script of Uncle Harry Oldroyd, my Aunt Dorothy's husband.

> Bowtawn Farm,
> St. Breward,
> Nr. Bodmin, Cornwall.
> 5th July, 1971

Dear Davey,

By now you will have received a copy of Petherick's Will from Mr. Thody. (I looked quickly across at my leather purse in which that precious document lay folded along with two other letters from Cornwall I'd received in the past week; but back to Uncle Harry from Lancashire).

You have probably heard from various members of the family, but your Aunty Dorothy wanted me to write before we appeal that ridiculous Will, as I was there at Petherick's deathbed and know exactly what state he was in. And as a member of the family by marriage only and with my personal experience on the Magistrates' Bench, what I have to say will have special weight in a court of law. The death wasn't very pleasant, Davey. Apart from the Parkinson's Disease, which as you know, he had for years, he had cancer of the bowel, too, before the end. I heard him say at least three times, while he was in the Nursing Home in St. Austell, that he ought to make a Will. He had obviously forgotten that silly bit of paper which benefited that crook Pengelly and which was produced after Petherick had passed on.

I should tell you, too, that Pengelly never once came to the Nursing Home. As your Aunty says, he was probably too busy going through Petherick's effects in the house, because all the womenfolk in the family discovered that there wasn't a bit of your Great Aunt Hetty's jewellery left. Not a trinket. And all the things she had promised your Aunty Dorothy before she died . . . in fact the poor woman must be turning in her grave, to think of those strangers prowling through her house thieving her things.

Your Cousin Jane, who has been poorly for so long and who wasn't even mentioned in that illegal Will, is now off her head in grief. You know what a favourite of Great Aunt Hetty's she was.

Your Aunty Dorothy particularly wants me to say we do not begrudge your being left the two-tenths — especially as Petherick was so fond of your dear mother. But we would appreciate a letter — send it to Mr. Thody — saying you are in agreement with all the family that it is an illegal Will and that Petherick would have been the last person in the world to leave what is rightfully ours to a complete stranger.

Yours in sorrow,
Uncle Harry.

P.S. Are you thinking of coming over? That would be the best, believe me.

" Are you coming up to the cottage for lunch ? " Tessa asks. " I want to show you a new walk I've found through the woods."

"Pass me my bag please, will you ? " I make the request as polite as possible, considering I'm ignoring her question.

She does as I ask and I take out the other two letters and the Will, deliberately smooth out their creases, lean back on the silver sand and hold up the letters to blot out the sun. I start re-reading them. The first is from the Reverend Trewin, an elderly clergyman, Vicar of our Parish after I had emigrated to Canada, and the last priest Petherick had known.

Dear Mr. Bryant :

Your Cousin's Will has come to my notice and your Cousin Leslie Trelooe, whose sight is failing, has asked me to write, agreeing my sympathy of protest against the outrageous terms. On my own behalf I want also to declare that in the thirteen years I knew your cousin as his Parish Priest I was wholly unaware of the gross perversion he nourished in his breast.

I am an old man, in my eighty-third year, and as one whose ministry has encompassed many decades, I can only say I was not only shocked by the discovery of Petherick Bryant's secret vice but would have reported him to the authorities (whichever relevant in these corrupt, permissive times) had I become aware of his abomination.

I am sure that as a blood relative you are properly aghast, sir, at this blatant attempt to misdirect family fortunes, but equally as a Christian man (I recall your presence many years ago at St. Endellion Church) you must be revolted by the discovery of a pervert within the sacred confines of family.

Thus apart from gladly acquiescing in your cousin Leslie's request to support the family in its claim, I would also like to accord you, sir, every sympathy in the revelation of a man given over to unnatural conduct and who once, in the wiles of his hypocrisy, had the gall to suggest himself as my Churchwarden.

If there is anything specific you care from me, please do not hesitate to write.

Yours truly,

Desmond Trewin, Parish Priest (Retired).

The other letter was briefer.

Dear Mr. Bryant :

I am sure you have heard — or will — from most of your relatives about old Ped's Will. It come as a surprise to me and the Missus as I really haven't seen much of the old chap these past years. But we had some fine old talks in the past and I knowed all along that in his funny way, he was brave and fond of yours truly.

What none of they do know is that he has been paying for our Sunday joint of meat, when Mr. Chapman of St. Tudy, come round with his butcher's van, every week since me and Shirley was married. That's eleven years come Michaelmas.

The money will come in real handy as I would like to farm for myself and not for Mr. Buse. And we have five youngsters here who cost a pretty old packet as you can imagine.

Do drop in if you ever come by this way and can tear yourself away from Canada where I hear tis proper cold. And I am glad you got the two-tenths as old Ped always talked nice about you. Which he never did about any of they.

Yours very truly,

James Pengelly.

" Anything the matter ? " asks Tessa.

Or did she ? It wasn't her I heard. Only the sighing wind through the telephone wires on the road from Pendogget to Polzeath and the mewing of blunt-winged buzzards as they soared above heathery cliffs.

My inner eye saw the soft grey of the granite in that Norman nave where Petherick lowered his large body to the hard wooden kneeler to pray. My nose caught the yeasty tang of bottled up centuries in Endellion Church and found it mixed with the damp and paraffin scent of the oil-lamp cottage where Petherick sat growing old without anyone to care. And ridiculous, sentimental me suddenly wanted to cry.

" I wish you'd tell me all about it, Davey. It's over a week now. That's why you came over from Vancouver, isn't it ? "

That brought me back. I blinked and forced a grin.

" It's nothing, sweety. Really. A kind of joke."

" Funny kind of joke. I called Ken, you know. He told me that someone had died. One of your folks in Cornwall."

" Ken should keep his blasted mouth shut."

" You and Ken fallen out, is that it ? "

Ken and me . . . fallen out . . . Why can't Tessa keep her hopes to herself ? Poor old Petherick . . . having spent a lifetime hiding his right hand from his left, now sending his jackal family howling, even as his carcass starts its quiet rot under the trees of Endellion Churchyard where they'd planted him.

I looked beyond her anxious face, avoided the sun, and stared for relief into the unblemished blue. Those weren't buzzards up there. They were eagles, loftily sailing. Then this wasn't Cornwall. This was Canada.

" Davey, where are you ? I wish to hell I could be there with you ! "

A last, longing look at the clear, clean mountains over Vancouver Island, and awareness of arbutus and salmon-berry tangled somewhere behind my back. Then the downward descent to rendezvous with those kind and large gray eyes.

" Hi, sweetheart! Like to answer a couple of questions?"

" Of course, Davey. You know, I'd do anything . . ."

" Here they are, then. How much is one where one **is ?** And how much is one where one **was ?**"

Then I settled back, my hair in the sand, drawing up my knees and closing my eyes, to await her dear, ridiculous answers to such vain questions.

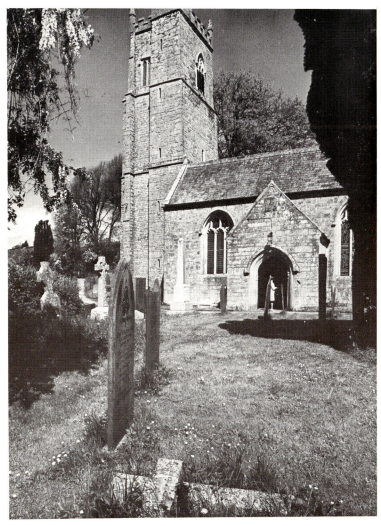

St. Kew Church

Photo : Ray Bishop

12msc   V59441

LONDON BOROUGH OF LEWISHAM
LIBRARY SERVICE

Author _____

Title _____

Books or discs must be returned on or before the last date stamped on label or on card in book pocket. Books or discs can be renewed by telephone, letter or personal call unless required by another reader. After library hours use the Ansafone Service (01-698 7347). For hours of opening and charges see notices at the above branch, but note that all lending departments close at 1 pm on Wednesday and all libraries are closed on Sundays, Good Friday, Christmas Day, Bank Holidays and Saturdays prior to Bank Holidays.